.50

GUNSMOKE LAW

GUNSMOKE LAW

GUNSMOKE LAW

Wade Hamilton

AVALON BOOKS

THOMAS BOUREGY AND COMPANY, INC.

22 EAST 60TH STREET · NEW YORK 10022

PUBLISHED SIMULTANEOUSLY IN THE DOMINION OF CANADA
BY THE RYERSON PRESS, TORONTO

PRINTED IN THE UNITED STATES OF AMERICA
BY THE COLONIAL PRESS INC., CLINTON, MASSACHUSETTS

GUNSMOKE LAW

GUNSMOKE LAW

Chapter One

WHEN tall Buck McKee reached the Matthews farm, he found the buildings in a heap of cold ashes. The homestead shack had been burned to its rock foundation, and the barn and other buildings were also down, victims of a fire. North of the burned-down house a few rods was a small mound of fresh earth, and the tough cowpuncher studied this with a frown, a cold feeling creeping along his spine despite the heat of the Montana day.

Was a child buried here? The grave was about that size.

The ashes told Buck that his old friend Matthews had run into trouble, and cold fear rode the Texan.

But there was nothing he could do here, so he turned his leg-tired sorrel north toward Yellowstone City, six miles away.

Suddenly he drew rein, belly freezing.

A man had unexpectedly stepped out of the buck-brush ahead, a Winchester under his arm. He was a short, tough-looking hombre who swaggered with the rolling gait of a horseman afoot.

"You lookin' for somebody—or somethin', stranger?"

A deep voice rumbled upward out of a very thick

7

chest. There was an air of toughness about this squat man, further accentuated by the .30-30 rifle.

Buck couldn't understand this. A half mile back he had seen a sign: *Wadsworth Matthews Farm,* and there had been no need to open the gate—the fences had been cut, lying in bits of shiny barbwire.

These cut fences had told him that Matthews had run into trouble. Then there had been the wheat field, burned to the sod, black and ugly against the Montana soil.

Buck had scanned the burned-down spread from a hill before riding down, but his field glasses had failed to pick out this hidden man.

"No," Buck said, "not looking for anybody, fellow. I'm just a stranger riding through."

"Then how come you ride off the main trail and look at this burnin'?"

Buck didn't like the looks of that Winchester. "Just curious, nothing else. Thought maybe, seeing there'd been a fire, I could help some person who had had tough luck."

"Be you a new farmer? One movin' in on Circle Five graze, maybe?"

Buck thought, So *that's* the core of the trouble, and he said, "Does a farmer come in on horseback, stranger?"

"How do you figger one comes?"

"He's usually got a wagon loaded down with farming equipment. He's pullin' a plow and some other farming implements behind the wagon, with a cow or two."

"You don't say."

Buck held his temper. "And most of the time he has his woman and kids in a buggy, mister. He don't ride in alone, a single man with his warbag tied to his saddle. Or does he?"

The rifleman scowled. Thinking seemed to come hard to him, and Buck forgot his anger, grinning inwardly. "Reckon that's right," the rifleman finally admitted.

"I'm no farmer," Buck McKee said, and that was the truth.

"Then what may you be?"

"That's my business, mister—and mine alone!" Buck spoke in a flat tone.

Anger momentarily flooded the thick face, then as suddenly disappeared. "I reckon you're right, stranger. Me, I'm not a-guardin' this burned-down outfit. I was riding in yonder draw lookin' for Circle Five cows when I saw you come over the skyline, so I thought I'd investigate."

Buck knew now why he had not seen this man through his field glasses. The man had been hidden over the ridge. Sudden fear clawed Buck McKee, chilling his blood.

And the fear was not for his own safety, but for the safety of his heavyset Mexican partner, Tortilla Joe. By this time, Tortilla Joe should be in this area, for he had also come to visit his old friend Wadsworth Matthews.

"Right neighborly of you," Buck said, "but what happened back yonder? Looks to me like some homesteader done got burned out."

"None of your damned business, savvy?" The rifle

barrel rose slightly. "Jes' keep ridin' on, stranger. Savvy?"

Buck had one boot loose in stirrup. For one moment, he almost launched that boot out, for then he would catch the squat man under the jaw. If the boot wouldn't drop the man cold, it would drive him back so Buck could leap on him. But then the worn blue barrel of the Winchester made a sharp gesture of dismissal, and Buck McKee wisely decided not to argue with a loaded rifle.

"You're not very friendly to strangers," Buck remarked.

"Nope, I'm plumb unfriendly—a mad porcupine with his quills up, stranger. There's the trail, gent. And at the other end of it is Yellowstone City!"

"Thanks for the information," Buck said cynically. He put his boot solidly in stirrup and trotted away, glancing back once.

The man stood there, rifle raised higher, watching him leave, and Buck waved cynically and rode toward Yellowstone City.

He talked to one other man before riding into the pioneer cow town, for he met a farmer about two miles down-trail. The hoeman and his wife were loading their heavy cookstove onto an old wagon.

When the farmer saw Buck, he hurriedly shoved the stove onto the wagon's bed and then reached for the twelve-gauge double-barreled shotgun leaning against the wagon's near wheel. He stood with sturdy legs spread wide, the endless torrid wind of August blowing his tattered overalls against his legs.

"Step back, Ma," he said.

The heavyset woman stepped to one side, fists knotted as she watched Buck ride in, right hand held high and palm out in Comanche peace pattern.

"I look for no trouble," Buck said, reining in. "I'm just a stranger riding through—so why the scatter-gun on me?"

The farmer panted from his labors. The stove was anything but light. Buck glanced at the wife, a thick and buxom woman dressed in a tattered gingham dress and worn apron.

A frame homestead shack stood behind the wagon. Two young boys came out of the cabin, each carrying an old chair. They stopped when they saw Buck, fear spreading across their faces.

"Be you a Twiggs's rider?" the farmer asked.

Before Buck could answer, the older boy said, "He don't ride no Circle Five horse, Pa. His horse is branded Bar F on the right shoulder."

The shotgun lost none of its rigidness. "Many a killer Circle Five man rides a hoss with a foreign brand, son."

Buck sweated more than the heat called for. "I don't know a thing about this Circle Five," he said. "Evidently, you farmers are fighting a cow outfit running that brand. I appeal to your reasoning, man."

"Keep talkin'," the farmer growled.

"If I were a Circle Five killer, would I ride down on you without a weapon in my hands?" Buck asked.

The man frowned. The boys shifted bare feet. The woman spoke for the first time. "He's right, Pa. Our nerves are shot, I guess, from rememberin' what happened to Wad Matthews night afore last."

"I'd be relieved, mister, if you pointed that scatter-gun in some other direction," Buck said gently.

"He's all right, Pa," the woman said.

The husband gingerly put the shotgun down, butt foremost, against a wagon wheel, his deep eyes riveted on Buck McKee. "Thanks, ma'am," Buck told the wife. His eyes went back to the stocky farmer. "Mister, what's this all about, anyway?"

"What d' you mean?"

"A few minutes ago I rode up to some burned-down buildings. A man who said he rode for Circle Five came out of the brush and challenged my right to be on that ground."

The woman listened. The boys stood in silence. The heavy man's deep eyes still regarded Buck.

"This Circle Five man threw a Winchester down on me," Buck said. "Now you up at me with that scatter-gun. That's twice in just a few minutes. Besides it being dangerous for me, I'm getting plumb inquisitive."

"That was Wad Matthews's outfit that got burned down," the older boy said, but Buck already knew that.

"Circle Five burned him out," the younger boy said.

"And Circle Five killed Mr. Matthews's pet dog," the older boy added.

The farmer said, "Hush, boys," and then, to Buck, "Circle Five hit Wad Matthews at night. They killed Wad's pet dog and made Wad bury the dog, with blood streamin' outa Wad, and him having to bury his best friend."

Buck remembered the grave. It held a dog, not a human. "Where's Matthews now? Was he killed?"

"No, he's down in Yellowstone City," the farmer said, "with a murder charge against him."

"Murder?" Buck's brows rose.

"Whitey Jordan got killed in the ruckus," the wife said. "Whitey slung a gun for Circle Five. Circle Five claims a Mexican killed Whitey."

Buck's heart sank. The Mexican *had* to be Tortilla Joe, his sidekick, for few Mexicans got this far north. With an effort, he kept his voice level. "What happened to the Mexican?"

"He never got hurt," the farmer said. "He's down in Yellowstone City, too, charged with murder."

Buck began breathing again. "Who owns Circle Five?" he asked.

"Ol' man named Twiggs," the husband informed him. "He owns the iron, but the big ramroddin's done by Twiggs's foreman, a killer named Rocky Pincus."

Rocky Pincus . . . Buck stored that name away carefully.

"Take a good lawyer to get the Mexican out of jail," the woman said, and Buck got a sudden idea.

"How about Wad Matthews?" Buck asked.

"He needs a lawyer, too," the woman said, "but he ain't in jail."

"Where is he?" Buck asked.

"He's in the town hotel, in bed. They had a little gun ruckus, you know. Wad got shot in the ribs."

"Right ribs," the man said. "Some broken, maybe —I don't know. He got shot in the leg, too."

"Left leg," the woman said. "And it's busted."

Buck had things clear.

"You a lawyer?" the woman asked.

"I'm a lawyer," Buck fabricated, and rode on.

Buck made one stop before riding into Yellowstone City—in a grove of old cottonwoods a mile outside of the cow town.

Here, a small spring bubbled out of the hill. First, Buck watered his horse; then he bathed as best he could in the small pool.

He took a new blue suit from his warbag, shook it out, and hung it on a branch; then he shaved carefully, using the pool as a mirror.

Afterward, he pulled on a clean white shirt and a blue tie, donned his suit, and polished his boots. He dusted off his hat carefully. The Stetson was new, having been bought down in Billings when he had ridden through that horse town.

He swung up on his horse, looking like the model businessman, his old range clothes in his warbag behind his saddle.

Soon he was riding down Yellowstone City's main street, his eyes missing nothing. Plank sidewalks. Dirty windows. False-fronted buildings. Dogs sleeping in the shade.

Then he saw the redhead.

Chapter Two

SHE stepped gingerly off the plank sidewalk into the dust, skirt held high enough to show a well-trimmed ankle. Even with a wealth of piled-up red hair, she wasn't over five feet tall, but she walked with the pride of a little princess.

Buck reined in and said, "Very dusty street, madam."

She had deep blue eyes. A light band of freckles ran across her somewhat stubby nose.

"Did I speak to you *first*, cowpoke?" Her voice held icicles.

"You're beautiful," Buck said.

The blue eyes momentarily showed something that looked like cordiality, then this became replaced by anger.

"Keep riding, waddy!"

Buck grinned. "Give me a woman with spunk," he told the world, and rode into the town livery barn, where he turned his horse over to the hostler. "Lots of oats and good bluejoint hay."

"Be in town long?"

"My business," Buck said pointedly, and looked up and down the main drag, thinking that if a man wanted to learn anything, he usually found it in a

15

pioneer saloon. Apparently, Yellowstone City had two such drinking emporiums.

On his side of the street a weather-beaten sign extended out over the boot-hammered plank walk: Broken Cinch Saloon. Directly across the dusty street from the Broken Cinch was another old sign, equally weather-hammered, that said: Wild Horse Bar.

Buck decided on the Broken Cinch, for it was closer. He noticed some saddled broncs standing hip-humped at the Broken Cinch's tooth-gnawed hitch-rack, but across the street in front of the Wild Horse were four rigs—three wagons and a buggy—and Buck figured that the cowmen patronized the Broken Cinch, while the farmers did their drinking in the Wild Horse.

He also noticed that the saddled broncs in front of the Broken Cinch bore the Twiggs's Circle Five iron.

Buck pushed through the Broken Cinch's batwings. The long saloon stretched ahead, with the bar on his right, and the center occupied by card tables and two pool tables.

At the bar were the bartender and five cowboys, two of whom shot a listless game of pool while two others played seven-up at a card table. The fifth man stood alone at the bar, his back to Buck as Buck entered.

This man at the bar was a neck-yoke wide across the shoulders. He stood an inch under Buck McKee's six-foot-one. He turned as Buck entered, and Buck noticed he was light as a cougar on his Justin boots.

Buck saw a wide nose, thick lips, and deep yellow eyes, and again he thought of a puma.

All eyes swung to Buck, a stranger. Buck went to the bar, nodding dutifully. "A bottle of your coldest beer," he told the bartender.

"Coming up, stranger."

Buck looked at the big man. The big man looked at Buck. "You're a stranger," the thick lips mouthed, "so state your business here in Yellowstone City."

Buck put a polished boot on the worn brass foot-rail. "You come straight to the point," he murmured. "But, by the same token, I could ask you what you're doing here and what your name is."

Anger stiffened the yellow eyes. "Know me as ramrod of Old Man Twiggs's Circle Five outfit. Mark me in your memory as Pincus—Rocky Pincus."

Buck thought, I've already marked your name, Pincus, and he summoned a smile, for he wanted information and not trouble. "McKee is the name, Mr. Pincus. Oliver McKee, attorney-at-law."

"Shyster, huh?"

All eyes watched Buck carefully. The pool players leaned on cues, the card players laid down hands. Buck only hoped he could somehow live up to his new role as a lawyer.

He remembered Deadwood, a town in the Black Hills of South Dakota. Three winters ago. . . . He and Tortilla Joe had spent three months that winter in the Deadwood jail.

The charge had been wrecking a saloon and Buck's beating up the town marshal. No lawyer would take their case because both had been penniless, but Buck had managed to get some law books from the county attorney to study, intending to plead his own case and his partner's when the circuit judge arrived in March.

But his study of grammar and law had come to naught. The sheriff had run him and Tortilla Joe out of Deadwood before the judge arrived. "Save the county money," the lawman had mumbled.

Now this big hard range boss had labeled him a shyster, and Buck knew the word shyster denoted a crooked lawyer. *Shyster* was a fighting word.

But Buck didn't want to fight, so he took the insult in stride, swallowing his pride to do so.

"Some call us lawyers *shysters*," he said, sipping cold beer, "but others don't. Each person is allowed his own opinion, Mr. Pincus. Very cold beer, bartender."

"You aim to set up an office here, McKee?"

"I might. I like the cut of your town, sir."

"Maybe Yellowstone City won't like your cut," Pincus said deliberately.

Buck realized this conversation was getting nowhere. Pincus had insulted him, and he, against his will, had accepted the insults. He heard one of the Circle Five cowboys openly snicker.

Buck lowered his beer. "I'll have to chance that."

"We've already got one lawyer here. He won't take cases for farmers, though. Works only for Circle Five. City attorney, too."

Buck nodded. "I seek only to make a legal living,

Mr. Pincus. I want no trouble. I look only for a place to practice. And to practice, I need clients."

A Circle Five cowboy laid down his pool cue. "He needs *practice,* huh? Why don't you let him *practice* on that Mexican, Rocky?"

Everybody laughed except Buck and Rocky Pincus.

"Or on that farmer what shot himself the other night," another cowboy said, "and who claims Circle Five burned down his homestead—the big liar!"

Buck turned his beer mug slowly on the mahogany bar, realizing he had gained his point. Conversation was now on Tortilla Joe and Wadsworth Matthews.

Buck asked innocently, "Do you men imply I have a possible client?"

"You have two," Rocky Pincus pointed out. "One is a Mexican, in jail for murder. The other is wounded—shot hisself, I guess—he's in bed in the hotel. He's also charged with murder."

Buck nodded.

"But neither of them has got forty bucks between them," Pincus said, "so they'll have to be charity cases . . . that is, if you take them on!"

"Who'd they kill?" Buck asked.

Pincus lifted his bottle. "Of course, all the details aren't clear yet, McKee, and won't be until the judge comes for spring court, which is quite a few months away, huh?"

"Almost a year," Buck said.

"As close as we can determine, this Mexican and this farmer set the farmer's buildings on fire, either on purpose or by accident, but everybody thinks it was done when they were drunk, and done on purpose to lay the blame on Circle Five."

Again Buck nodded.

"Well, about the time of the fire a Circle Five cowboy named Whitey Jordan—darn fine boy—rides by the farm and sees the fire and apparently rides in to help the Mexican and the farmer put out the flames, and I'll be darned if that Mex and that farmer don't kill poor Whitey in cold blood!"

Buck felt a cold spot hit his belly. Circle Five really had Tortilla Joe and Wadsworth Matthews railroaded.

Buck's memory skipped back five years to the time he and Tortilla Joe yad been railroaded in Elko, Nevada, on a murder charge.

They had been pounding nails into the gallows when Wadsworth Matthews had braced his saddler against a rope and pulled out the jail bars. Wad had had horses staked out, and the three of them— Wad, Buck, and Tortilla Joe—had fled Nevada.

The trio had broken up in Colorado, Wad riding north and Buck and his Mexican partner heading south for their old stamping grounds around Mesilla, New Mexico Territory.

Somehow the three had kept track of each other through the years. Now Wad was wounded and under arrest, and Tortilla Joe, whom Buck hadn't seen for six months, was now in jail.

Buck had his work cut out. Now, musing and listening to Rocky Pincus's deep voice, he wondered why Circle Five, powerful as it was, hadn't broken into the hotel and the jail and strung up Wadsworth Matthews and Tortilla Joe.

Circle Five could do it, too, and never be brought into court, because plainly Old Man Twiggs's big outfit bossed this northern Montana range, like feudal kings whose word was law.

"Doesn't look like a lawyer'd have much chance," Buck now told Pincus. "Open-and-shut case for Circle Five, looks like."

"County shouldn't have to feed and house those two," Pincus said shortly.

Again an icy ball formed in Buck's belly. Pincus could mean but one thing: a howling lynch mob, a jail and hotel delivery, and two bodies hanging in the dawn, necks broken. . . .

"I'll look into this case," Buck said, "but doubt if I'll take it. Where there's no money, there's no use working, huh?"

"Right," Rocky Pincus said.

Buck paid for his drink and left. The sun was still brassy hot. He headed for the courthouse, a frame building down the street, and met the beautiful girl with the red hair. He deliberately stepped in front of her.

The redhead had changed to a light summer dress, and despite the heat, she looked very, very cool—and very, very competent.

She stopped, scowling angrily. "Are you in the habit of taking up all the sidewalk?" she asked icily.

"I'm Oliver McKee, attorney-at-law."

"How romantic," she said cuttingly.

"And your name—?"

The full lips tightened. "My name maybe is Olivia MacKee," she said cynically, "with the *Mc*-Kee spelled with a *Mac,* maybe?"

Buck stepped aside. "You win."

She continued on, red head held high. Buck spoke to a small boy playing marbles in the shade. "What's her name?"

The boy looked at the redhead's lovely retreating back. "Her?" he said. "You interested in her?" He didn't wait for a reply. "That's high-toned Marcia Andrews."

"*Miss* Marcia or *Mrs.* Andrews?"

The boy shot a marble and missed. "She ain't married. Nobody'd marry her. She's too high-toned."

Buck glanced back at Marcia Andrews. To his surprise, she entered the Broken Cinch Saloon.

He scowled. Decent women didn't go into saloons. He rubbed his smooth-shaven jaw, then shrugged and went on to the courthouse.

Chapter Three

SHERIFF Jenkins was a middle-aged, heavyset short man who wheezed with each breath. "You're a lawyer, huh? And you want to see the Mex? Can't be done, Maginnis."

"McKee," Buck corrected. "*Attorney Oliver Mc-Kee.*" He liked the sound of *Oliver*. He had thought of it on the spur of the moment. It sounded more high-toned than *Buckshot*.

He only hoped he would run into nobody he knew on this high northern Montana range except Wad Matthews and Tortilla Joe. But he realized he had little to fear: he had never before ridden this section of Montana.

But recognition was a chance he had to take.

"You can't see the Mex," the fat sheriff wheezed.

"The Mex—as you call him—is guaranteed legal representation under the Constitution of the United States of America," Buck said.

Sheriff Jenkins scowled. "Maybe I'd best ask the county attorney. You sit down and don't move outa this office, savvy? I'll trot back down the hall and consult the attorney."

Buck sat down. The sheriff left, still wheezing. The small office smelled of magazines, dirt, mice, and gunpowder.

A gun rack hung on the far wall. It held some rifles, a few sawed-off riot shotguns, and Tortilla Joe's worn gun belt, complete with .45 bullets and the Mexican's trusty Colt .45 riding low in the well-oiled holster.

Right now, Buck figured, Tortilla Joe wished he had that gun. He glanced up as a very short and wide man, wearing brown range clothes, sauntered in, a deputy sheriff's badge glistening over his heart.

"Deputy Sheriff Isaac Watson," the man said. "What can I do for you, stranger?"

"Not a thing."

"What d'you mean?"

The thick man's arrogance irked Buck, but he held his temper as he explained his being there. At that moment, Sheriff Jenkins wheezed back into the musty office.

"Attorney says you can see him, but I have to be with you when you two confer," Sheriff Jenkins said.

"I'm sorry," Buck said, "but under the Constitution I am free to consult my client—or possible client —in private, with nobody present."

"The Constitution says that?" Jenkins asked.

"Check your attorney again," Buck said.

"This gink's a lawyer, huh?" Deputy Sheriff Watson spoke to Sheriff Jenkins, who only nodded.

"Maybe the Mex doesn't want a lawyer," Sheriff Jenkins said. "Let's talk to him and see if he does, Mr. McMahon."

Buck made no effort to correct the sheriff. He and the lawman went along a stone floor to a cell row at the back of the building. Buck ran a quick and appraising—and practiced—eye over the jail proper.

This section of the courthouse was made of solid stone, firmly cemented together. The cell area consisted of four cells. Buck only hoped that Tortilla Joe, upon seeing him, would not call out his name in surprise.

But that, too, was a chance he had to take.

Tortilla Joe was the only prisoner. His strong hands gripped the bars of the cell. Buck deliberately walked a pace behind the panting sheriff, and so Jenkins didn't see the tall Texan quickly lay a finger to his lips and motion Tortilla Joe to be silent.

Tortilla Joe understood immediately. "Who ees thees man you takes there, Sheriff?"

"He can't even speak good English," Sheriff Jenkins rasped to Buck. He turned to Tortilla Joe. "This gink here claims to be a lawyer. He wants maybe to take your case, savvy?"

"Oh, an *abogado,* huh?"

"What the hell is that?" the sheriff asked suspiciously.

"*Abogado* ees the name for lawyer, in *Mexicana.*"

"This is the United States," Sheriff Jenkins said shortly. "Learn to speak a good language, Mex. You want a lawyer, or don't you?"

"I got no monies."

"We can talk that over later," Buck told his partner. "My name is McKee. *Oliver* McKee."

"The pleasure she ees mine, *Señor* McKee."

"Okay," Sheriff Jenkins said. "He wants you for a shyster, MacWilliams. Now talk."

"I demand that my client and I have complete privacy—just the two of us—when we discuss his case," Buck said. "I demand that you go and question your attorney on this point."

"Forgit it," Sheriff Jenkins growled. "I'll jes' search the prisoner after you leave. Have a nice long talk, boys."

The sheriff left, bootheels echoing on the stone floor. Buck looked into Tortilla Joe's cell, heart sinking. The cell hadn't a single window to pull the bars out of!

Tortilla Joe opened his mouth to speak, but Buck

again held his finger over his own lips. "Sheriff hasn't shut the door to his office yet," Buck hissed.

"He leaves it open all the time."

Buck called out, "Sheriff Jenkins, your office door is open, sir. You can hear our conversation, I feel sure."

"Okay, shyster."

The door closed. Tortilla Joe gripped both of his partner's hands. "I didn't think you'd ever come, old buddy." Now that he and Buck were alone, Tortilla Joe spoke good English. "They're railroading Wad and me like they did you and me down in Nevada!"

"Only difference is that this cell ain't got no windows," Buck said. "I know the details. Circle Five hit Wad's shack, burned it and the outbuildings. Who killed this Whitey Jordan skunk?"

"Wad killed him. We had quite a fight. I saw Wad pull down on this Whitey with a rifle. Wad got Whitey through the heart, first shot."

Buck nodded.

"Wad killed him and they all saw it and they charged me with murder, too. Is that justice?"

"Circle Five justice," Buck said, "and it's a wonder a necktie party hasn't staged a jail delivery and lynched you both."

"You make me feel so happy," Tortilla Joe said. "Do you think you can pull off this pretending to be a lawyer?"

"Remember Deadwood? And the heap of law books I read there?"

"I remember it too well. I've been trying to forget. I hope nobody here recognizes you."

"You've got company there!" Buck grinned.

"Where'd you get the new suit?"

Buck and Tortilla Joe had split up last May after winterfeeding A Lazy V Bar cattle down in Colorado, Buck going into Idaho to punch cows for Old John Sturdivant's N Bar N outfit, and Tortilla Joe going south into Arizona Territory to visit relatives and ride herd on Gila River cattle.

"Got in some good poker games in Idaho," Buck said, "and won some dough. You still aim to winterfeed cattle with me up in Canada for the Heart Bar Six outfit?"

"We got the job, for sure?"

"Got a letter in Idaho from Jack Carter, asking that I bring you into Alberta with me; so I wrote to you in Arizona, and then you wrote you'd meet me here because we both intended to visit Wad—but what the hell, I'm only repeating what we both know."

"And Carter said we had a winter-long job?"

"Yeah, but I got to get you out of jail first. A man can't dole bluejoint hay to bawling dogies if he's behind bars." Buck rubbed his jaw thoughtfully. "Have you and Wad had a preliminary hearing?"

"Yeah, before the j.p. here. He set our bail at twenty thousand dollars."

"Well," Buck said, "we can't get you out on bail. Together, you and me will never have that much money in our whole lives."

"Bust me out?"

"How?"

"I don't know," Tortilla Joe said. "This jail has

no windows. And if you dynamite a wall—well, I'll be killed inside."

"How's Wad?"

"Wad is loco, Buckshot. And I mean that."

"Watch your tongue!" Buck said sharply. "Forget the *Buckshot* or *Buck!* Play it safe, Tortilla. Call me *Mr. McKee,* savvy?"

"I forgot. But we are alone."

"It isn't now so much as you might make the mistake later. What'd you mean, Wad's crazy?"

"He is not the man we knew. He was married, you know. His wife ran out on him a year ago. He's been here two years. He's in love with his dog."

"Oh, talk sense!"

"He and the dog lived alone. Now they killed the dog. They made him bury the dog that night when his house burned."

Buck scowled. "He saved our necks. We got to save his. I've got a derringer in my pocket. But I can't smuggle it to you now. The sheriff said he'd search you and your cell."

"What we going to do, Mr. McKee?"

"I'll talk to Wad. I'll think of something. Hang and rattle, friend." Buck wheeled and left.

Deputy Sheriff Isaac Watson had left the office, but Sheriff Jenkins had a visitor, and the beauty of this visitor made Buck McKee's blood quicken.

"Mrs. Twiggs, this is a new lawyer what just rode into town, name of McFee."

"Mr. Oliver *McKee,* Mrs. Twiggs, and the pleasure is mine, madam."

"How interesting," Mrs. Twiggs murmured. "And

the sheriff told me that you already have two clients
—the Mexican, and the farmer who is shot and in the
hotel."

"I haven't made up my mind yet," Buck said.

Sheriff Jenkins said, "I'm going back to search the
prisoner. You stay here, McKee, until I come back."

"Okay, and for once you got my name right."

"Huh?"

"I'll be here," Buck said.

Sheriff Jenkins wheezed, scowled, and left, the
sound of his bootheels ringing back.

Louise Twiggs perched on the corner of the desk,
idly swinging a leg encased in a sleek bucksin riding
skirt, a silk stocking, and a highly polished small
Hyer boot with a silver-mounted spur.

Buck was puzzled. He judged this blonde beauty
to be no more than around twenty-four, and he had
heard that Old Man Twiggs was a bedridden an-
cient. Had Twiggs a son or two, and was this beauty
Old Man Twiggs's daughter-in-law?

He decided to try something.

"I understand the farmers and your father-in-
law are having trouble, Mrs. Twiggs?"

"Father-in-law? Old Man Twiggs is my husband,
Mr. McKee."

Buck noticed that the woman picked nervously at
the leather fringe of her split riding skirt.

"Oh, I'm sorry," he said.

"Mr. Twiggs—Old Man, as he's called—is my husband."

"He seems to be successful in running out the
farmers," Buck said.

Mrs. Twiggs stuck out her finely shod foot and studied it carefully. "So I understand," she murmured. She lifted calm blue eyes that appraised Buck carefully. "Do you intend to stay here in Yellowstone City, Mr. McKee?"

"The town appears very attractive to me."

She laughed throatily. "You are not a very good fabricator, sir. Even a blind man could see that this town is ugly."

Sheriff Jenkins returned. "No weapons left with the prisoner or in his cell," he wheezed. "You can go now, Mr. McLean."

Buck lifted his hat to Mrs. Twiggs and turned, bumping into a boy who had barged into the office. The boy was the one who had told him Marcia Andrews's name.

"Rocky Pincus says for you to see him right away in the Broken Cinch," the boy panted.

"Why?"

"I don't know. You gotta ask him."

Chapter Four

BUCK paused momentarily on the plank sidewalk in front of the Broken Cinch, eyes moving across the street to the Wild Horse, where three men—plainly farmers—stood and watched him.

Then he entered the saloon.

The Circle Five men were again the saloon's only occupants, outside of the bartender, who leaned his beefy hands on the bar and stared at Buck as he entered.

Rocky Pincus had his back to the bar, whiskey glass in hand, and Buck saw that the man was drunk, for his lips were loose, his eyes narrowed and scheming.

"You wanted to see me?" Buck said.

"I've made up my mind," Rocky Pincus said. "This town don't need you, McKee. You be on your hoss and headin' out inside of ten minutes, savvy?"

"No more than ten minutes?" Buck asked.

Pincus studied him, sobering rapidly. "You heard me," he said. "Ten minutes."

"I just told your boss—over in Sheriff Jenkins's office—that I liked it here," Buck said.

"My boss? He ain't in the sheriff's office. He's home at the ranch—in bed—"

"Mrs. Twiggs," Buck informed him.

Rocky Pincus snorted. "She ain't my boss! Are we seeing eye to eye, shyster?"

"We are not," Buck assured him.

"Then you aim to stay?"

"I do."

"Go out in the alley, men," the bartender said. "For Lord's sake, don't bust up my joint, please!"

"This won't be fists," Rocky Pincus told the barkeeper. "He's got a gun strapped to him, and so have I."

Cold reality stabbed Buck McKee. Pincus had

lured him into a trap. He faced five Circle Five gun-hands. Concentrated gunfire from five guns could kill him. And no questions would be asked. Circle Five owned this town and could do what it wanted.

He had not expected this. He had expected Rocky Pincus to make gestures toward him, but none this deadly and serious. He realized he could take one or possibly two Circle Five gunmen with him, but he would never come out of this alive.

He heard the batwings swing open behind him. He moved to one side, sliding on the balls of his boots, so he could watch the door and the Circle Five killers at the same time.

Mrs. Twiggs had entered. She moved back, put her lovely back against the wall, and said nothing. Rocky Pincus stared at her.

"What're you doing here?" the range boss demanded.

"Public place," the blonde said.

Pincus's thick lips made swallowing motions as he tried to fit Mrs. Twiggs into this situation. "This won't be nice to look at," he told his boss's wife.

"What won't be, Rocky?"

"You know what I mean. You're not that dumb!"

"I can be very stupid," the blonde said, and added, "at various times, that is!"

Rocky Pincus glared at Buck McKee. "We ain't got nothin' to talk about, McKee!"

Buck didn't understand all this. He caught an edge of dislike toward each other in the voices of Rocky Pincus and lovely Mrs. Twiggs, or was his imagination working overtime?

A hundred thoughts flitted through his mind. Had the woman deliberately entered this beer-smelling saloon to see that he had a fair chance?

If so, this meant that Mrs. Twiggs was against Rocky Pincus, for if she had favored Rocky, she would have let him—Buck McKee—walk into Circle Five's roaring guns.

"I think you're wrong, Pincus," Buck said. "I think we *do* have something to talk about."

"Like what?"

"Like your threatening me a minute ago, before Mrs. Twiggs entered."

"No gentleman uses a gun in front of a lady, McKee."

"We don't need guns. We've got fists, haven't we?"

Buck's logic was simple. Rocky Pincus had challenged him before the eyes of Yellowstone City. The other time he had been in this saloon, Pincus had ridiculed him and his new-found profession. Buck knew that if Pincus were allowed to get by with this, Yellowstone City would have Buck McKee labeled as a coward.

Buck knew these pioneer towns. Once a man showed a white feather, that man was through. He had no love for Yellowstone City. To him, Yellowstone City was only another stinking dust-blown prairie cow town, nothing more.

He would stay in Yellowstone City just long enough to see that Tortilla Joe and Wadsworth Matthews escaped the hangman's noose of Circle Five. When he rode out of this Montana town, he expected Tortilla Joe—and maybe Wad Matthews—to ride with him toward a winter job across the line in Canada.

"I can break you in two!" Rocky Pincus snarled.

Buck sent a glance over the big man, and wondered if Pincus was right; Pincus outweighed him at least by twenty pounds, and looked strong and tough as a Hereford bull.

"Come and do it!" Buck challenged.

"You two idiots," Mrs. Twiggs said as Rocky Pincus shuffled forward, fists up in his best prizefight manner.

Circle Five riders set up a happy yelp, calling encouragement to their foreman, while the bartender screamed for somebody to stop them, claiming in a loud voice that his bar would be wrecked.

Buck moved forward to meet Pincus, a happiness surging in his veins, remembering how this arrogant cowman had insulted him but a few moments before.

They circled, Buck waiting for Pincus to lead; Pincus, with his head down low, growling curses. Then Pincus shot out a left—and Buckshot McKee went to work.

Sliding under Pincus's blow, he counterpunched with a left, letting the foreman's fist slip harmlessly over his shoulder. His left jarred hard and rigid into Pincus's beefy face. He rocked the heavyset foreman back on his spurs, and Pincus grunted in pain and surprise.

Buck crossed with his right, knuckles smashing the side of Pincus's face, and he dropped the foreman with two blows.

Rocky Pincus landed sitting down in a sprawled heap, blood trickling out of his mouth.

"Good Lord," somebody gasped. "McKee dropped him with two blows!"

"An' Rocky ain't never been knocked down afore," another man said. "An' he's won every fister he's been in!"

"Get up, you big pig!" Mrs. Twiggs said. "Fight for the honor of Circle Five, you slob!"

Her sarcastic tone registered on Buck. He glanced at her. She had a short-barreled .32 pistol in her hand pointing down at the splintered wooden floor.

Buck circled, fists ready. Slowly, carefully, Rocky Pincus pulled his strong, muscular legs under him, his eyes on Buck.

Buck didn't know whether Pincus intended to get to his feet or to launch himself ahead in a tackle, and he judged the former—and here he erred.

Without warning, Rocky Pincus lunged ahead, arms spread wide in a football tackle. Buck leaped to one side . . . too late. Pincus's huge arms fastened tight around Buck's knees.

Buck went back hard against the wall, then hit the floor. Rocky Pincus dropped his tackle quickly, sitting astraddle Buck, his huge fists hammering Buck's face.

Salty blood touched Buck's tongue. Somehow he rolled, pitching Pincus back; somehow he got both boots in the foreman's guts and kicked with all his might.

Pincus gasped. Buck's boots smashed into the range boss's belly. Pincus went back, stumbled, fell; when he came up, he held a chair. Swiftly Buck also grabbed a chair.

"Come on!" he gritted.

He heard wood crash and break. What the heck—? He glanced to his right. He saw a man, a stranger, bounce a chair off the head of a Circle Five man.

The Circle Five man staggered backward. With one leap, the stranger was on the rider, jerking the cowboy's gun and throwing it aside.

"Get 'em, farmers!"

Then Buckshot McKee understood, remembering the three farmers who had stood across the street in front of the Wild Horse Bar when he had entered the Broken Cinch.

The farmers had joined the fray.

But Buck had his hands full with Rocky Pincus, who was far from dropping out. Pincus roared in, chair lifted; Buck leaped to his right, burying the legs of his chair in the foreman's belly.

Pincus's chair missed, hitting empty air. Buck's chair drove the range boss's breath from his husky, saddle-tough body. For one moment, Pincus bent . . . and that moment was enough.

Buck McKee's chair came down. The thick wooden rim of the seat crashed down across Rocky Pincus's neck, just below his skull. Pincus never knew what hit him.

He lunged ahead, out on his feet, and crashed headfirst into the bar, his enormous weight sending the bar toppling. Bottles crashed from the back bar, and the bartender screamed even louder, but Rocky

Pincus, now lying on his back, arms spread out, didn't hear the barkeeper . . . or anybody else.

Breathing heavily, spitting blood, Buck McKee straightened—and then, from nowhere, a man leaped on his back.

The lunging blow almost drove the winded Buck to his knees. Somehow he managed to hold his footing. Blows rained down on his unprotected head. Huge spur rowels gouged his tender midriff, tearing his new shirt.

A Circle Five cowboy had mounted Buck as though he were a bronc, spurs digging, a wild yell on his cracked lips as he hammered Buck's head.

At first, Buck McKee didn't know what to do. He had never been caught in a similar situation before. Then he remembered how Rocky Pincus crashed headfirst into the bar.

The cowboy astraddle him, Buck lowered his head and ran for the wall. He stopped just before slamming into the planks, his head down, body bent low.

The cowpuncher astraddle Buck crashed, headfirst, into the wall. Buck felt the spurs leave his belly. He pulled back fast and the man, knocked cold, fell off his shoulders.

The man landed on the floor, rolled over, and lay still. Buck recognized him as one of the Circle Five waddies who had been playing pool. Buck whirled, fists up, head pulled down, ready for fisticuffs, but nobody rushed him at this moment.

The saloon was a riot. Men slugged, cursed, fought. Another Circle Five hand rode a farmer. The farmer bucked like a bronc, but the cowboy stayed on him, smashing blows onto the hoeman's head.

Mrs. Twiggs had her small six-shooter raised. Buck figured that she hoped to slug the farmer, but to his surprise, she was trying to lay the steel on the Circle Five rider.

Breathing hard, Buck wondered why she hoped to slug one of her own hired hands. By rights, she should be angling to lay the farmer cold.

She stood on tiptoe behind the cowboy, trying to get a clean swipe at his head. Buck glanced hurriedly around. The two other farmers were slugging it out with two cowboys.

Buck didn't like this a bit. The whole thing was unnecessary. Besides, it proved nothing. It didn't help get Tortilla Joe out of jail, or have the murder charges lifted from Tortilla Joe and Wadsworth Matthews.

He heard yelling outside. He whirled, seeing faces at the broken windows. A flash of brilliant red hair was visible, and he knew that Marcia Andrews was watching.

Where were Sheriff Jenkins and Deputy Sheriff Isaac Watson? Surely by this time they had heard this ruckus and had come to investigate, but he could see neither of them anywhere.

He understood then. Circle Five was in this fight. Circle Five paid the wages of the sheriff and the deputy. Neither lawman had come, because to have done so would have gone against Circle Five.

He turned and looked at Mrs. Twiggs. The lovely

blonde, at this moment, had a clean shot at the cowboy's head. Her pistol came down, barrel first.

By sheer luck, the cowboy unconsciously jerked his head to one side. Mrs. Twiggs missed. Her pistol barrel thundered down on the farmer's head instead, dropping him in his tracks.

"I hit the wrong one!" she said. Then, to Buck, "McKee, behind you—"

Maybe she completed her sentence. Maybe she didn't. Anyway, Buck McKee never heard the rest.

He whirled . . . too late. When he came to, his throbbing head lay in a woman's lap. He looked up at lovely red hair.

"Hello, sweetheart," he foolishly told Marcia Andrews.

Chapter Five

BUCK stared at the man in the bed.

When Tortilla Joe had said that Wad Matthews had changed during the last few years, Tortilla Joe had not exaggerated. To Buck, looking at the former cowboy, it seemed that this was a new man—not his old pal Wad Matthews.

Only the voice was the same. "Darn glad you could come, Buck. What happened to your face?"

Buck told him about the fight in the Broken Cinch. "Now you're on the side of us farmers," Matthews said.

Buck had realized the same thing. And what was more, he didn't like it. He hadn't asked the farmers to pitch into the Broken Cinch battle. They had barged in of their own accord, and thereby had made it look as though he were one of their members. He had not wanted sides in this range war.

"What happened to you?" he asked.

"Me? You've heard, haven't you? Tortilla Joe got in three days ago. Night afore last, Ol' Man Twiggs's Circle Five hit my holdings."

Buck waved a hand. "I know that. You and Tortilla are charged with murdering one Circle Five waddy, one Whitey Jordan. Tortilla told me you really killed him."

"I did, Buck. And I'd kill him again if I had the chance."

"Look, Wad, I'm not *Buck* McKee here. I'm *Attorney-at-law Oliver* McKee." Buck told the farmer about his deception. "How come a deputy or somethin' ain't out in the hall guarding you?"

Wad Matthews laughed bitterly. "Where could a gink go with a busted leg, Buck—I mean, Oliver? You really getting by with this lawyer thing?"

"I hope so. I might be able to work it, might not. Can we raise bail for you and Tortilla Joe?"

"What'll we use for money?" Wad Matthews asked. "You got that much?"

"I haven't. . . . You've lost weight. You look much older."

"I got married in South Dakota. Took my wife here. She pulled out on me about a year ago."

Buck said nothing. He had known other men who had separated from their wives but had never lost weight. "How many other farmers have been shot at or burned out?"

"None. I was first. Give me a gun, McKee! For Lord's sake, man—leave your gun with me!"

"You'd gain nothing by shooting your way out of this," Buck said. "And they'd find the gun and take it away."

"McKee, I need a gun!"

"How come Pincus picked on you?"

"I don't know, McKee. He's always had it in for me. Maybe he hates me because I was once a cowpuncher."

"That don't make sense," Buck said.

"Well, the other farmers—there's about a dozen—they've always been farmers. They were farmers back in Indiana and Ohio and the other states they come from."

Buck nodded.

"Circle Five's made fun of me on the sly, callin' me a cowboy who's gone bad, and junk like that."

Buck nodded again. This was, to him, small talk—surely, the problem was deeper. Anyway, this Matthews was not the same Matthews who had torn him and Tortilla Joe from a Nevada jail. Something more serious than a bad marriage had happened to Wadsworth Matthews.

What could it be? Buck wondered.

"What's goin' on here?"

The rough voice came from the doorway behind Buck. Deputy Sheriff Isaac Watson stood there.

"Talking with my lawyer," Wad Matthews said. "I got the right to have counsel, Deputy."

"I demand that my client have law protection, Deputy Watson," Buck said. "Circle Five can sneak in any time and kill him."

"You don't say," Watson said cynically. "Be just another damned farmer gone, and no loss."

"How much does Old Man Twiggs pay you each month?"

Deputy Sheriff Isaac Watson's ruddy face went beet red. "You got too much lip, McKee!" he growled. "They've judged shysters, too, you know—and this town is sort of open-and-shut, too!"

"What do you mean by *that?*" Buck asked.

"You figure it out!" the deputy said. He turned to Wad Matthews. "I take it you and Mr. McKee have finished your conflab?"

"We have," Matthews said.

"I'm filing an affirmation with the county attorney," Buck said. He had no idea what an affirmation was, and he knew Watson knew less. The name, though, sounded big and legal.

"Affirmation for what?" the deputy asked.

"I'm stating in this affirmation that if my client here, one Wadsworth Matthews, is killed while confined to bed, then in my opinion he has been murdered by some Circle Five man who has sneaked in and dispatched said Wadsworth Matthews."

"What good'll that do?" the deputy sheriff wanted to know.

"Montana law states that the county attorney will have to file this affirmation in Public Records," Buck fabricated. "A copy must also be sent to the circuit judge of this district."

"Circuit judge, huh? Hey, no need to go to all that trouble, Mr. McKee! I'll talk to my boss right away. He'll have a guard posted over this prisoner in no time!"

"Good day, sir." Buck left.

He had learned something. When he had mentioned the name *circuit judge,* the deputy had immediately changed his tune. Evidently, this jurist was an honest man? And local county officials feared him?

Buck went slowly down the old stairway to the lobby below, where he rented the room next to Wad Matthews before going outside into the falling dusk.

Heat clung to the rangelands. August was probably the hottest month here, Buck guessed. But the range didn't suffer from lack of moisture.

He had seen only one better cow range, which was the Big Bend country of West Texas. Here, bluejoint grass stood high on a horse. The Circle Five cattle he had seen on his ride in had been butter fat.

Milk River held plenty of water, and so did its tributary creeks. Springs ran back in the foothills. Circle Five cattle had plenty of the two things necessary to raise fat steers: lots of grass and plenty of available water.

He heard a door open in the building behind him, which was the Andrews Drugstore. He turned. Marcia was closing her store, key in the lock. Her cold, cynical beauty made Buck say, "Thanks for helping me after that Circle Five cowboy slugged me cold, Miss Marcia."

"Think nothing of it, Mr. McKee."

Buck admired her slim lovely beauty, there in the dusk. "I wonder why you put my head on your lap. Weren't you afraid you'd soil your dress?"

"Don't be cynical, Mr. McKee."

"I'm still wondering," Buck said.

"The doctor said your head should be up a little when he poured that dram of whiskey down your throat. So I sat down, put your head on my lap, and thereby raised your head higher."

Buck moved closer to her and detected a faint scent of perfume. She moved back further into the doorway. He had her penned in the corner. Nobody else could see them.

"What do you want?" she said huskily.

"You sometimes go into the Broken Cinch?"

"I do. But isn't that my business?"

"I might be old-fashioned, but I thought only one type of woman went into saloons."

"I like to play poker. Is there a law against a woman playing poker?"

"Not that I know of."

"Mr. McKee, why have you penned me in? If I cried for help, a dozen men in this town would tear you apart. My father started this store before I was born. He died last year. He came into Montana from Texas with Old Man Twiggs. My name—and character—are much respected on this range."

"You apparently dislike Mrs. Twiggs very much."

She studied him with level eyes. "Why do you say that, Mr. McKee?"

"Mrs. Twiggs was also in the Broken Cinch when I came to with my head on your lap. I heard words pass between you. To me, those words didn't sound very cordial."

"You imagine things, Mr. McKee. Louise Twiggs and Old Man Twiggs have been married since Louise was sixteen, and that was eight years ago. She and her father came through town with a medicine wagon. Apparently, she and Old Man Twiggs immediately fell in love. They married right away, and Louise's father drove on alone."

Buck stepped back.

"You're a strong man, Mr. McKee. But really, you have nothing at stake here, now have you?"

Was she fishing for something? "I don't follow you," Buck said.

"Come now, Mr. McKee. You're an attorney, a learned and intelligent man. Neither this Mexican nor this farmer has any money. And you work for money, don't you? Gratitude fills no tables. I know that. I foolishly overextended credit to these farmers."

"Are you advising me—warning me—to move on, Marcia?" Buck asked softly.

Her laugh was molten silver. "Mr. McKee, what an imagination! Pray, what difference would it make to me if you made a complete ass of yourself over an ignorant farmer and a more ignorant Mexican?"

"You are right," Buck said.

"A smart man would move on," the redheaded woman said. "And you are an intelligent man, Mr. McKee."

Buck lifted his hat. "I thank you. Might I walk you home, Miss Marcia?"

Again that silvery laugh. "I live over my store. All I need do is climb the stairway on the side there, open my door—and I am home. But I thank you, Mr. McKee."

She passed him, dress rustling, perfume still clinging, and then she stopped and looked at him. Her smile was haunting, yet cynical, and she said, "Good night, Mr. McKee."

"Good night," Buck said.

She climbed the stairway, dress held high to show beautiful ankles, and then she was gone.

Buck heard a door open upstairs, and close.

He stood there in the gathering darkness for a long moment, tension thick in his lanky, wiry body.

He would have to break Tortilla Joe out of jail. Each moment his Mexican sidekick spent behind bars was a moment fraught with great danger for the jovial, good-natured son of Old Sonora.

Why had Circle Five hit at Wad Matthews and not any other farmer? Why pick on Wad?

What were the stakes in this deadly game being played in this rolling sagebrush country? When men fought and killed and died, they did these things for tangible items such as land or water or cattle or graze. But apparently this range held plenty of land for all. Water was not in short supply. Were farmers stealing Circle Five cattle?

Deputy Sheriff Watson left the hotel and spotted Buck still standing in front of the drugstore. "Mr. McKee, I'm going to the office. I'll talk with the sheriff. A guard will be over pronto to sit with Matthews."

"You've said that before."

Watson stopped, looked at Buck, and said, "McKee, you're hard to get along with," and he sent a slow, careful glance up and down the main street, breathing heavily.

Buck McKee felt the gnawings of hunger. He said, "Me for the cafe and—"

He never completed his sentence.

The roar was loud. Buck knew instantly that a six-shooter had gone off in a closed area like a room. The roar came from upstairs in the hotel.

"What the—?" Deputy Sheriff Watson said.

Already Buck was on the run for the hotel door. He collided with the screaming clerk in the lobby.

"A shot—upstairs—in Mr. Matthews's room—"

Heart hammering, Buck took the stairs three at a time. He landed in the hall. It was empty. He turned left, running toward Wad Matthews's room.

The door was open. A kerosene lamp burned low. Matthews was lying on his back, the bed covers down around his waist. His right hand held a smoking .45.

Buck McKee stared at his old friend. All the blood had drained from Wad Matthews's face, leaving it gaunt and gray.

The bullet hole was below Wad's right ear.

Chapter Six

BUCK stared in amazement. Something was loco here. Wad Matthews had begged—yes, implored!—for a gun. And all the time he had had a gun under his bedding!

Had Matthews been lying? Had he had a six-shooter with him while begging for another?

Or had somebody slipped in while Buck had been down on the sidewalk? And had that somebody given Matthews this gun?

Suddenly a thought hit Buck. Surely the hotel had a back entrance. He ran down the hall and jerked open a door. He looked down on a wooden staircase leading into the alley.

Nobody moved in the alley below.

Buck realized that by now an assassin had had time to escape. If Wad had been murdered, the murderer had come up this stairway. He had not come in from the front. The hotel clerk would have seen him, and so would he and Deputy Sheriff Watson.

Buck hurried back to Wad Matthews's room. Deputy Watson had sent the clerk hurrying for the sheriff.

"My God, you smuggled him a gun, McKee!" the deputy snarled. "I arrest you, here and now!"

"Talk sense," Buck said. "I've got but one gun and

it's in my holster, Deputy! Maybe somebody sneaked in—killed him—forced that gun in his hand—"

Deputy Sheriff Isaac Watson snorted. "Of all the harebrained ideas—! How do I know you never packed another gun?"

"Sheriff Jenkins searched me when I went back to talk to the Mexican," Buck reminded him. "He'll verify that I had only one gun then."

"But you might have got another?"

"Where?" Buck asked angrily. "I've stood enough of this, Deputy!"

"You might stand more, shyster," the deputy growled. "Here comes the sheriff."

The hall was filled with townsmen attracted by the noise and the shooting. Sheriff Jenkins, his face red, hammered his way through them and finally got into the room.

"What happened?" he wheezed.

"Watson'll tell you," Buck said.

While Watson recited the details, Buck picked up Wad Matthews's limp arm. No gunpowder marks were on his hand. Buck scowled as he noticed that the skinny arm was marked with fresh little sores, looking much like mosquito bites, only a trifle bigger.

Buck's eyes narrowed.

Night had fallen. He borrowed a lantern from the desk clerk and started for the back alley.

"What the heck you doin'?" Sheriff Jenkins demanded.

"Going to scout," Buck said. "Maybe somebody slipped in and murdered Wad. There might be tracks back in the alley. We know he never came in the front way."

"He had a gun hid out," the sheriff said, "and he took his own life."

"Who's guarding the Mexican?" Buck asked.

"The jailer. He's got a shotgun, short-gun, and rifle. Why ask?"

"You figure it out."

The lantern's dim rays showed many tracks in the alley of man and beast, mostly dogs. Buck searched carefully at the staircase's landing, but saw at least eight different sets of boot and shoe prints.

Marcia Andrews saw his light and came down. "Widow Mattson told me about it. Isn't it terrible?"

Blue house slippers encased her tiny feet. A red dressing gown hugged her small waist and accentuated her full-blown femininity.

"Tough," Buck murmured.

"You lost a client," she said.

"That's so," Buck said.

"What are you looking for in this alley?"

"I just lost my favorite marble," Buck said. "My best shooter."

She stared at him. "You're crazy, Mr. McKee." And she walked off, leaving a grinning Buck McKee behind.

Finding nothing in the dust, Buck blew out the lantern and placed it inside the hotel's back door. He then went down the alley to the sheriff's office and the county jail.

The jailer sat beside the door leading to the cells,

a deadly shotgun over his knees. "What'll it be, Mr. McKee?"

"Just checking," Buck said.

"Nobody can get back to the prisoner," the jailer said. "Them's the sheriff's official orders."

Buck realized Tortilla Joe was safe. The Mexican's cell had no windows. The only access to Tortilla Joe was through the door the jailer guarded, and down the corridor behind the door.

Buck dropped into the Broken Cinch. The bartender had straightened up the bar and swept out broken bottles and righted tables and chairs. He glared at Buck.

"Not my fault," Buck said. "I never started it."

"You should be across the street with the farmers," the bartender said. "In the Wild Horse. This saloon is for cowboys, Mister Lawyer."

Buck ordered a beer. "You get me wrong. I've got no love for hoemen."

"Then how come they come roarin' in here to help you when you had the ruckus with Circle Five?"

"You got me," Buck said. "I never met one of those men before. I guess they figured they'd side with me because Wad Matthews was my client—and a farmer."

"*Was* is right," the bartender said. "I wish you'd leave, McKee. Sometimes Circle Five cowboys ride in for the evening. The home ranch is just a few miles north of town, you know. And I sure don't want this joint wrecked again."

"You seem to be a good guy," Buck said. "Do you

mind telling me who bent his pistol barrel over my thick skull?"

"You don't know?"

"Haven't asked anybody but you, so far."

The bartender's big hand mopped the bar with a damp towel. "Sooner or later somebody'll tell you, so I might just as well. You was beaned by Blacky Jordan, a young Circle Five waddy."

"Blacky Jordan," Buck repeated. "He any relation to Whitey Jordan, the one killed at Matthews's fire —the Circle Five man they claim the Mexican and Matthews killed?"

"Twin brothers, shyster. Blacky is the light-haired one. Whitey had hair black as ink. You know, for brothers, they sure didn't love each other."

"What d'you mean?"

"Them two fought each other all the time. They fought with fists, clubs—you name it, they used it."

"Guns, too?"

"Nope, they was never let go that far. Once on a roundup—last fall, it was—they got into a ruckus and went for their irons, but Rocky Pincus grabbed Whitey and another Circle Five cowboy downed Blacky before they could drag iron on the other."

"Whitey got killed instantly, they tell me."

"Yep, shot right through the heart. They say that Matthews aimed right at him and then Whitey fell dead."

"Was Blacky at the Matthews's fire?" Buck asked.

Suddenly the bartender's voice hardened. "Look, shyster, you just ask too many questions, an' that ain't healthy for you or for me. Them farmers is waitin' for you in the Wild Horse acrost the street, remember."

"I guess I'll have to quit drinking," Buck said.

"Why?"

"Well, if I have to drink in the Wild Horse, the farmers will figure for sure I'm on their side, and I don't want them to figure that way."

"Okay, come in here when no Circle Five is here. And if Circle Five comes in while you're here, you go out the back door. I never want to be accused of driving a man to sobriety, shyster."

"Thanks," Buck said.

Buck downed his beer and went to the Antlers Cafe, where he got a side table and sat with his back to the wall, listening to the natives gossip about Wadsworth Matthews's death and the trouble riding this long-grassed northern Montana range.

Suspicious, quick glances were shot his way, then past him. He realized he was a figure of some conjecture among these people. The thought amused him, even though he occupied his mind with the riddle of Wadsworth Matthews.

Although he wasn't positive, he believed that Matthews had been murdered. He had made an error that he couldn't correct at this moment. He had suspected a killer of sneaking in the hotel's back door. Actually, the killer might have come from one of the other rooms on the second floor.

Sheriff Jenkins entered, looked about the cafe, then saw Buck and pulled a chair up to his table.

"Coroner's inquest at ten in the morning, about the corpse of the deceased Wadsworth Matthews," the lawman wheezed. "You'll be there, of course, Lawyer McKee?"

Actually, it wasn't a question. It was an order.

"I'll be there," Buck said. "What does it look like to you, Sheriff?"

"Suicide, of course. Matthews had that gun hid somewhere, maybe in his mattress."

"How did he get it there, and where did it come from?"

Jenkins's wheeze momentarily disappeared. "I'll be blunt, McKee. Things look bad for you. You saw the prisoner alone. You might have slipped him that gun!"

"Let's not jump into the dark," Buck said. "Let's identify that .45 first. Was the .45 that killed Matthews his own gun? Or does the Colt belong to somebody else? If so, to whom does it belong?"

Sheriff Jenkins's wheeze returned. "You've got strong points, shyster. But when Wadsworth Matthews was arrested, his .45 was taken from him. It now hangs in my office."

"The gun and belt and bullets hanging from the rifle rack?"

"No, those belong to the Mex." Sheriff Jenkins frowned. "Where the hell did Matthews's gun belt and pistol go to? My Lord, they used to hang on that rack, too!"

"You mean, somebody stole them?"

"I don't know. Maybe Watson put them in the safe. I gotta check on that. Lord, if a man doesn't do a thing himself, it never is done right, huh?"

Buck cut into his prime T-bone steak and didn't answer. He had no idea he had been this hungry.

Deputy Sheriff Watson came in, hooked a chair, sat down, and told his boss that the body of Wadsworth Matthews was being taken to the jail, to be locked in a cell until morning.

"He killed himself with his own gun," the deputy said. "He had his initials—W M—on the butt."

"How'd that gun get outa the office?" Sheriff Jenkins asked, again not wheezing.

The deputy shook his head. "I don't know, Sheriff. I never even noticed it was gone, did you?"

"Not until the lawyer here pointed out that only one gun and belt hung on the rack, and I know they belong to the Mex. I had a hunch you'd put Matthews's hardware in the safe."

"I never did no such thing," Deputy Watson said, looking at Buck. "You didn't sneak thet hardware out when you visited the Mex this afternoon?"

Buck studied the squat deputy carefully. "One more accusation out of you, Watson, and I'm trimming your wick with either my fists or my gun—and I'll give you your choice."

Watson's jowls reddened with anger. He half rose from his seat, but Sheriff Jenkins reached out and pushed his deputy down again.

"Don't make a fool outa yourself in public, Watson," the sheriff hissed. "McKee never had no chance to get that hardware. He was watched every minute he was in the office."

Deputy Watson spoke softly to Buck. "I might take you up on that offer, shyster."

Buck got to his feet, his meal finished. "I'll be around for several days," he assured him. "Good night, gentlemen."

He paid the girl, and just then a group of towns-people crowded out the front door, blocking it, so he decided to go out the back door.

He came out into the dark alley. The cafe was set about ten feet from an adjoining dark building. To reach the main street and his hotel, Buck had to go through this narrow path.

He never reached the plank sidewalk. He heard boots rustle behind him, and, hand snaking to his pistol, he tried to turn—too late.

Dark night fell on him.

Chapter Seven

THE next morning, Buckshot McKee was breakfast-ing in the Antlers when Mrs. Twiggs slid onto the seat opposite him. "How do you feel this morning, Mr. McKee?"

The lovely young blonde wife of Old Man Twiggs was an appealing figure in a white blouse and Sioux-fringed buckskin riding skirt, her small feet encased in polished Justin half boots.

"I want to thank you for your help last night," Buck told the beauty. "I'm not used to being knocked cold twice in one day. I found this in the pocket of my pants this morning. I missed it last night when you helped me to my hotel room."

He handed Louise Twiggs a note printed laboriously in pencil on a scrap of brown wrapping paper.

"I saw you leave this cafe by the back door last night," Old Man Twiggs's wife said. "I guess you didn't notice me in the bunch that came in late for coffee. That's how I came to find you unconscious. I wanted to talk to you. We never had a chance, your being in the condition you were in."

"Read that note first, please."

She read aloud: "Get out of town fast and stay out and don't come back." It was signed, "Circle Five Ranch."

She handed back the note. "I know one thing," she said. "My husband didn't have a thing to do with sending you that note—or knocking you out."

"You spoke very highly of your husband last night, too," Buck said. "May I ask a personal question?"

"Certainly."

"Do you love your husband?"

The answer came immediately. "With all my heart, Mr. McKee. I know my husband is more than double my age, but I love him like I could love no other man. And I loved him the moment I laid eyes on him."

"May I ask another personal question, Mrs. Twiggs?" The lovely blonde head nodded. "How old is your husband? I've never had the honor of meeting him, you know."

"He was fifty-one last month."

Buck McKee scowled. This didn't make sense. Everybody referred to Old Man Twiggs. Buck had expected the Circle Five owner to be in his seventies, at least.

"How long has he been sick?" Buck asked.

"He's been bedridden for about a year and a half. He became sick two years ago. Before that, he was healthy as a horse."

"What does the doctor say?"

"This town has no doctor. The closest doctor is at Malta, almost a hundred miles away. I wanted to send for him, but my husband says no."

"Who treats your husband?"

"My husband has some very queer ideas. He takes medicine from a Sioux medicine man who comes to see him once every six months."

Buck's brows rose.

"My husband was reared by the Sioux. His folks were killed when he was a baby in a team runaway, and the Sioux took him and reared him. Then he went into Texas and somehow got enough money to get a trailherd and return to Montana."

Buck sipped hot coffee. Despite two bumps on his head, a night's sleep had cleared his brain.

"In those days it was possible to raise a trailherd down in Texas with very little cash. All a man had to do was to hire a few punchers for ten dollars a month and run wild cattle out of the brush. That was right after the Civil War. Texas was full of unbranded wild cattle then."

Buck nodded. His father had got his start in that manner, moving his trailherd onto the Texas Panhandle.

"Has your husband ordered Circle Five to run out farmers?" Buck asked.

Louise Twiggs twisted her coffee cup slowly. "Really, I can't say yes or no, Mr. McKee, because I don't know. My husband has few lucid moments, you know."

"Who administers the medicine the Sioux leaves behind for your husband?"

"Miss Marcia Andrews."

Buck remembered then that Miss Marcia owned the town drugstore, and in many pioneer towns the druggist also administered medicines. "You and Marcia don't get along very well," he said.

Louise Twiggs's face stiffened. "We just don't see eye to eye. I sometimes criticize the drugs—or whatever it is—she administers to my husband, but she says she is following the Sioux's instructions to a letter."

"Something is wrong here, Mrs. Twiggs. Seriously wrong. Perhaps you can tell me what it is?"

To Buck, it seemed that the beautiful blonde had momentarily hesitated, but when she spoke, her voice was firm, and Buck realized he could easily have been in error.

"I really don't know, Mr. McKee. I do know that apparently Circle Five is intent on getting rid of the farmers, and that Rocky Pincus is heading the drive."

"I'd still like to talk to your husband. I'd like to talk him into dropping the charges against the Mexican, because, after all, the Mexican is my client and a murder charge faces him."

"You are free to come to Circle Five whenever you like, Mr. McKee. I must get along now. I just rode in to see how you were, sir."

Louise Twiggs got to her feet. Buck also stood up. He bowed and she left. As she mounted her pinto he saw her through the cafe's front window. She lifted her hand slightly and galloped away, firm in the saddle.

Buck sat down. Within a minute, Sheriff Jenkins wheezed in and sat opposite him. "Coroner's inquest in twenty minutes in my office."

"Who's coroner?"

"I am."

"I'll be there."

"They tell me Louise Twiggs just left after talking to you."

"You heard true," Buck said. "I hope to have her husband drop charges against my client, the Mexican."

"Rocky Pincus signed the complaint," the sheriff pointed out.

"I'm sure Mr. Pincus signed in the name of Circle Five," Buck said, "and I feel sure any order by Mr. Twiggs would cancel Mr. Pincus's signature."

Sheriff Jenkins scowled. "I'd have to consult the county attorney on that," he wheezed. Then, without warning, he added, "I wish this thing could be dropped. I don't like trouble. I'd like to legally set this Mexican free. That Whitey Jordan—he was no good."

"What d'you mean by that?"

"Him and his worthless brother, that Blacky. Always fightin'. Causin' me trouble."

"Blacky slugged me," Buck said, wondering who had slugged him just last night.

"Who told you that?"

"There's no need to tell names," Buck said.

"You aim to get even with Blacky?"

Buck got to his feet. "I say neither *yes* nor *no*, Sheriff. Time we got to the coroner's inquest, isn't it?"

"Yeah, it's that time," Sheriff Jenkins panted.

The coroner's inquest was much as Buck figured it would be. Six old town drunks sat on the jury. The county attorney, a slat-thin, middle-aged man, sat to one side looking at Buck McKee, who testified along with Deputy Sheriff Isaac Watson.

Buck wanted nothing to do with the county attorney. The man might shoot some legal question at him that he couldn't answer, and the county attorney might then judge Buck McKee to be the fraud that he was.

No mention was made as to who owned the gun that had killed Wadsworth Matthews, Buck noticed. The verdict was what he expected. The jury was out but eight minutes.

"Suicide," the jury foreman intoned.

"Inquest dismissed," wheezed Sheriff Jenkins.

Buck hurried to leave, but the county attorney called, "Oh, Mr. McKee," and he and Buck shook hands, with the attorney telling Buck how glad he was to have a fellow attorney in Yellowstone City. Had Mr. McKee rented an office yet?

"Living out of my suitcase at the moment," Buck said, "and I'm sorry, sir, but I must leave your presence because of a former appointment."

"We shall meet again, Mr. McKee."

Buck hurried out, sweating in the heat. Quite a few farmers were in town. Rigs and wagons lined hitchracks on the east side of the main street, the saddlers of the cowboys were on the west side, and quite a few Circle Five men were in town, too.

Buck knew the farmers wouldn't start to harvest till the middle of September, when wheat and barley would be ripe. Cowboys would start their fall beef roundup about the same time. Therefore, this was the slack season for both hoeman and horseman.

A bunch of Circle Five cowboys loafed in front of the Broken Cinch, Rocky Pincus among them. They watched the people leave the courthouse after the coroner's inquest. Buck noticed that the Circle Five cowboys who had been in the Broken Cinch when he had fought Pincus were also in the group.

Apparently, all business establishments in town except the saloons had closed for the inquest. Marcia Andrews, lovely and trim, came along, red hair shimmering in the bright sunlight.

"Which one of those cowboys is Blacky Jordan?" Buck asked the lovely druggist.

"The young man there with his hat pushed back. The man with the blond hair."

"Thanks."

Marcia continued on toward her store, but Buck's never gave me a chance, either," he said. "I got your who had been shooting pool yesterday when Buck and Rocky Pincus had tangled.

The Circle Five men were loud and boisterous. One said, "I need a drink," and the gang trooped into the Broken Cinch, Rocky Pincus bringing up the rear.

Buck grinned, crossed the street, and entered the saloon. The bartender's eyebrows shot up. " 'Member our agreement, McKee?" he growled.

"I'll be in for just a minute," Buck said. "I lost my watch fob somewhere today, and I thought it might have dropped off my watch in here."

"I ain't seen it. What's it look like?" the bartender asked.

"Five-dollar gold piece on a leather band," Buck said. "Present from my grandfather."

"Five bucks," a Circle Five rider said. "That's worth lookin' for!"

The Circle Five men were at the bar, Blacky Jordan standing on Rocky Pincus's left. Blacky bent his head to look behind the footrail into the spit-trough for the gold piece. And at that moment Buck McKee slugged Blacky Jordan.

Rocky Pincus hadn't stooped to look, so Rocky saw it all. Buck McKee's pistol left leather in one swoop, and steel cracked skull bone.

Blacky Jordan's Stetson flew off, and he lurched ahead, out on his boots, and fell over the footrail, nose in the slop of the spit-trough.

Buck hefted his gun, looking at Rocky Pincus. "He never gave me a chance, either," he said. "I got your note, Pincus. Found it in my pocket this morning."

"What note?"

Buck laughed. Pincus wore a gaudy red silk neck-cloth, one end dangling, Buck caught this neckcloth with his left hand. Before Pincus knew what was happening, Buck had unceremoniously jerked Rocky Pincus forward.

"What the—"

Pincus never finished his sentence. Once again, Buck McKee's heavy Colt .45 chopped down. Again steel kissed skull bone. Pincus fell over Blacky Jordan. And Rocky Pincus never moved.

The whole thing had happened so suddenly, the rest of Circle Five was caught flat-footed. Buck backed toward the front door, his six-gun covering the surprised cowpunchers.

He dug into his pocket with his left hand. He came out with his pocket watch. From it dangled a leather watch fob with a five-dollar gold piece on the end.

He paused in the doorway, gun level. "Shucks, I didn't lose my watch fob after all," he said.

Then he was gone.

Chapter Eight

THAT afternoon, Lawyer Oliver McKee visited his client, Tortilla Joe. Again the tall Texan and the short Mexican talked without a third party in attendance.

Buck had had a length of spot-cord rope in his sad-dlebag. Before going to interview his client, he had wrapped the rope around the calf of his left leg. After the interview he rode toward Twiggs's Circle Five ranch. No spot-cord rope was wrapped around his leg.

He rode along a fence on the inside of which was a nice stand of barley, ripening in the sun, blowing under the slight wind. Buck liked its wonderful smell. He met the owner of the field plowing an-other patch for planting next spring.

"You're McKee," the farmer said. "I saw you in town this morning. I thank you for siding with us farmers."

"I don't understand, sir."

"Well, you helped Wad Matthews, God bless his departed soul, and Wad was a farmer, so you helped all us hoemen."

Buck sighed. "Don't get me wrong," he said. "I am, by profession, an attorney-at-law. I am for the law all the time, as my oath requires. That means I am im-partial."

The farmer shook his head stubbornly. "Nobody can stay on the fence here, Mr. McKee. Three farm-ers helped you fight Circle Five yesterday. You knocked out Pincus and that Blacky Jordan today. Anybody against Circle Five is for us farmers."

Buck felt a sense of futility. "Okay, as you say," he said, "but it seems odd that Circle Five has jumped only Wadsworth Matthews."

"Us farmers've talked about that, too," the hoe-man said, "and it seems odd they picked on Wad first, 'cause in a way him and Circle Five were friendlier than the rest of us farmers are with Circle Five."

"Will you elaborate, please?"

"Well, I know of a number of times when Wad drank with Rocky Pincus an' Circle Five in the Broken Cinch, the only farmer to ever do a thing like that."

"Maybe that was because Wad used to be a cow-boy."

"Mebbe so, but us others mentioned it more than once."

"Did you know Mr. Matthews's wife?"

"Yeah, I knew her. I know a man should always say good about other people, but, so help me Hanner, I can't say good about her. She was a good-for-nothin' female if there ever was one. Her and Wad fought all the time. She even went to a few dances alone, and she danced most of the time with Rocky Pincus."

"Where'd she go to?"

"Nobody seems to know, Mr. McKee. She was here one day, gone the next. Wad was sure lucky to get rid of her."

Buck rode on, adding this up. It didn't jibe with what Wadsworth Matthews had told him. A woman had entered the case, and Buck knew that when a woman was involved, there would be more trouble.

About a mile from the Twiggs's Circle Five he met Marcia Andrews riding a blue roan toward Yellow-stone City. She pulled in, riding a sidesaddle, and her brows rose. "You seem to be heading in the wrong di-rection, Mr. McKee. You're riding toward Circle Five."

"That I know," Buck said. "Perhaps I intend to

apologize for slugging down Blacky Jordan and Rocky Pincus."

"Mr. McKee, there are times when I doubt your sanity."

"And I too doubt that, Miss Marcia."

Buck remembered Louise Twiggs saying that Marcia doctored Old Man Twiggs. Evidently, the lovely druggist was now returning from Circle Five after riding out to give medical attention to Circle Five's sick owner.

He decided to say nothing about his knowing she doctored Old Man Twiggs.

"Rocky and Blacky are at the home ranch," the redheaded woman informed him. "Both nurse sick headaches. You have a very delicate touch with a six-shooter, Mr. McKee."

"Thank you," Buck said.

"Neither Blacky nor Rocky has a cut scalp. They have swollen spots, yes—but not a trace of a cut."

"You've inspected their scalps?"

"They asked me to. Sometimes I act as a sort of medical doctor, too. My druggist work, you know."

"I hope I get sick soon," Buck said, "because I want you to doctor me. You're a lovely woman."

For once, the redheaded woman smiled briefly—a fleeting expression, nothing more.

"I must hurry on, Mr. McKee. My drugstore is closed while I'm gone. I do wish you luck at Circle Five."

Buck lifted his hat. "Again I thank you, Miss Marcia."

The redhead loped toward Yellowstone City, sitting on her sidesaddle easily.

Within a few minutes, Buck rode around the toe of a hill and saw the Circle Five buildings ahead on a flat, the long rambling stone house covered with wild roses. A creek meandered through the spread, and Buck saw a bunkhouse, a cookshack, a blacksmith shop, three big barns, and a scattering of pole corrals.

He had seen beautiful spreads before, but this was one of the prettiest. He single-footed his horse along the wagon trail and soon rode into Circle Five's yard.

Two sleek and well-groomed collies came out barking, dancing around his nervous horse. This was the slack season in ranching, the time after spring calf roundup and just before fall beef gather, and most of Circle Five's cowhands were at the home ranch, checking gear and getting ready for beef roundup.

Somebody hollered, "Here comes the shyster!"

"Ridin' in bold as day," another waddy cried.

Men came running from the bunkhouse and the barns. Rocky Pincus headed the waddies, Blacky Jordan's boots pounding the spurs of his range boss's.

The dogs barked loudly.

"Get down, you dogs!" Rocky Pincus ordered.

The collies instantly quit barking, and slunk toward the house. Rocky Pincus bowlegged forward, tough and big, and grabbed Buck's reins in one hand, holding them hard just above the bit, and stopping Buck's horse.

"What d'you mean, shyster, by ridin' into Circle Five like this?" the foreman demanded.

"Drop my reins," Buck said.

Rocky Pincus grinned and tightened his grip. Buck's horse pawed the earth, wanting to move on.

"What're you doin' here?" Pincus demanded.

"You're right-handed, aren't you?"

Scowling, Pincus looked at Buck. "Sure I'm right-handed. What're you drivin' at?"

"You hold my reins with your right hand," Buck pointed out. "That means you can't pull your gun unless you've practiced drawing and shooting with your left hand."

"You wanta shoot it out with me?"

Buck shrugged. "Why not? You're slow with a gun."

"You ain't never seen me draw," Pincus growled.

"No, but I've fought you with fists. And you're awful slow with your dukes, so I know that you're slow pulling your gun."

"I can change hands on your reins, McKee!"

Buck shrugged. He glanced at Blacky Jordan. The youth's hard eyes met Buck's. For one long moment, Buck McKee's calm eyes locked with the young cowboy's slitted, ugly eyes. Blacky Jordan was the first to look away.

"You don't take him, I will," Blacky Jordan told Rocky Pincus.

"You're slower than Rocky Pincus," Buck said. "The only way you'll fight is to sneak in behind a man and slug him. Maybe you'd shoot a man through the heart if you knew he couldn't shoot back at you, huh?"

Blacky Jordan's face paled. "McKee, you'll eat

those words—" and then he stopped, for Louise Twiggs's calm voice, coming from the yard, said, "That's enough, you Circle Five men. I invited Lawyer McKee to this house."

She walked toward the group, lovely in a gingham housedress, her apron clean and fresh and gaily colored.

Blacky Jordan and the others, except Rocky Pincus, quickly doffed their hats. Pincus still held Buck's reins. Louise Twiggs halted ten feet away.

"Mr. Pincus, you undoubtedly have poor hearing. I told you I invited Mr. McKee to Circle Five."

"Ma'am—"

"Mr. Pincus, you seem to forget one thing. My husband owns this ranch. I am his wife. He is ill. I am therefore in command. And I command you here and now to take your hands from those reins."

Not for one moment did the blonde woman raise her voice. Buck noticed, though, that her blue eyes were chips of winter ice. Slowly, grudgingly, Rocky Pincus released the reins.

"This ain't finished yet," the Circle Five range boss told Buck McKee.

Buck sighed. "How many times have I read those same words—*this ain't finished*—in a Wild West book."

Pincus stepped back, wiping his right hand on his chap's leg. Buck dismounted and walked to the house with Louise Twiggs.

"He's a surly dog," the blonde said angrily. "Did you meet Marcia Andrews on the road?"

"I certainly did. I haven't spent my years in one

place, Mrs. Twiggs. I've met quite a few women. But I say here and now that I can't remember meeting one before that seemed as cold and ruthless as Marcia, if you pardon me for saying so."

"She pays attention to no man. She never has, I understand. She's self-centered and aloof."

"What does she seem to want in life?"

They were at the rail fence encircling the stone ranch house. Wild roses climbed the rails. Buck opened the wooden gate for Mrs. Twiggs, who entered slowly, apparently giving his question deep thought.

"I'm sorry," Buck said. "Marcia Andrews is nothing to me, so overlook my question."

"No, it's a good question, Mr. McKee. I'd say she wants only one thing: money."

"Money?"

"Yes, she seems money mad." They entered a huge living room with a stone floor and a wide stone fireplace at the far end. On both sides of the fireplace were well-filled bookcases. Bearskin rugs covered the floor. The furniture was made of sturdy native pine, and showed years of wear.

"This way, please, Mr. McKee."

They crossed the room and entered a long hall with doors on either side. Louise Twiggs stopped at the last door.

"Remember what I told you," she whispered. "My husband has lost much weight. He is no more than a scarecrow. He presents a rather frightful picture to a stranger, I would think."

Buck remembered the dead Wadsworth Matthews.

He had presented a rather scary picture, also, compared to his physical appearance when Buck had last seen him.

Mrs. Twiggs knocked lightly on the door. "Darling, there is a man to see you—a new lawyer, a Mr. Oliver McKee."

Buck and the woman waited. Buck heard no stirring beyond the door. Again the woman knocked, called, and a man's voice said shakily, "I want to see nobody. Lawyers mean nothing to me. Let me lie in peace."

"Darling, please. . . ."

Again the thin voice. "I don't want no doctor. I don't need no doctor."

"I said a *lawyer,* not *doctor.*"

"Preachers are all the same to me. I don't wanna see no preacher."

Louise Twiggs looked at Buck, her eyes deep and appealing, and then she opened the door and she and Buck entered.

Mrs. Twiggs had been right. Her husband was no more than a skeleton. His eyes were sunken dark marbles under shaggy, overhanging brows, his long nose hawkish and thin, his mouth thin-lipped and drooling.

Mrs. Twiggs took a handkerchief and wiped her husband's mouth. The room was big, light, and airy. Buck thought of wasted Wadsworth Matthews. He walked to the big window, below which was a flower bed.

He idly noted that the flower bed had recently been

spaded and raked flat. He turned and walked back to Old Man Twiggs's bed. He introduced himself.

The sunken eyes regarded him. "I never have liked businessmen," he muttered.

Buck came to the point, knowing his ride to this ranch had been wasted time, for this man was deep in insanity's grip. He asked Old Man Twiggs to drop the murder charge held against Tortilla Joe. "Never heard of anybody even gettin' killed," the rancher said. "What're you doin' here, anyway?"

"What do you mean?" Buck asked patiently.

"This section of West Texas don't need another schoolteacher," Old Man Twiggs said.

Buck talked slowly, patiently, trying to get through to the cowman, his heart cold inside. He got nowhere. Old Man Twiggs pulled his scrawny arms from under the covers.

Buck had a moment's start. The rancher's arms were pitted with small scars, like mosquito bites. He remembered Wadsworth Matthews's arms.

The rancher spoke to his wife. "My doctor? Where is he? I need medicine."

"He'll come soon," Louise Twiggs promised.

Despite the day's heat, the frail body suddenly began to shake. "I—need—my medicine. . . ."

Buck had a lump in his throat. He said, "Good day, sir," and while Louise Twiggs rearranged her husband's bedding Buck walked to the window.

Again he glanced at the flower bed, but his lack of interest soon died. Evidently, a man had crouched below the window listening to the conversation inside this room, for boot marks now showed on the raked soil.

Hurriedly, Buck scanned the area. He looked out on a strip of grass, and then at the rail fence. The collies played on the lawn, but no human was in evidence.

The eavesdropper had heard him say good day to Old Man Twiggs, had taken this as his cue, and apparently had quickly slipped around the corner of the house and disappeared.

"I want my doctor—"

Buck and the worried wife left. "What does he mean by *doctor?*" Buck asked.

"Rocky Pincus. He gives him hypodermic injections from medicine left by Marcia Andrews."

"Is that how his arms got those marks?"

"Yes."

Buck went to his horse, a heavy feeling inside him. Mrs. Twiggs called to Rocky Pincus, who stood in a group in front of the bunkhouse. Buck turned and rode back toward Yellowstone City.

Two miles out of town he met a mounted posse. Sheriff Jenkins, on a lathered gray horse, headed it, followed by a strawberry roan bearing Deputy Sheriff Isaac Watson, and a half-dozen townsmen strung out behind.

"McKee," the sheriff said, "you seen anything of this Mexican, your client?"

"I visited him in his cell today, remember?"

"He broke out about a hour ago. Somebody said he headed this way on foot."

Buck scowled. "I don't understand, sir."

"Well, I was alone in the office, see," the sheriff said, his face getting red, "and he calls for me and asks me to come with some rollin' tobacco, which I does. And when I turn to leave, he snags out with something, catches me around the throat, and chokes me down, with my back against the bars."

"What'd he use to garrote you with?" Buck asked.

"I don't get that word *garrote*. Talk white man's English."

"Snag around your neck and choke you down," Buck explained.

"I dunno. Might have been his pants leg. He choked me down like a cowboy chokes down a bad horse with a lariat. Of course, I had my cell keys on my belt."

"Good Lord, I'm without a client, huh?"

"We'll get him. We checked town. No horses has been stole. He's on foot. We searched town for him, never found him. I'm the laughin' stock of Yellowstone City."

"You seen a man on foot?" Deputy Watson asked.

"You know, I did see a man lugging along on shank's mare, about twenty minutes ago. He was over along the south hills there."

Everybody turned in his saddle, looking at the low ridge of grassy hills to the south, some three or four miles away.

"I could just see him," Buck said, "and I wondered why a man walked and didn't ride, and then I got thinking maybe it was a Circle Five man moseying around a water hole, his bronc out of sight in the brush."

"Let's head that way," Sheriff Jenkins said.

The posse wheeled and thundered south. Buck rode on toward Yellowstone City, remembering the boot prints in the flower bed. He also remembered Rocky Pincus's boots, when Louise Twiggs had called for him to go to Old Man Twiggs's bedroom.

Pincus's bootheels had held a rim of mud.

Chapter Nine

BUCK McKEE sat on the edge of the bed in his cheap hotel room and studied Tortilla Joe, who slouched in an old easy chair across the room.

"Your friend the sheriff told me he didn't know what you used to choke him down with. He figures that you might have dropped your pants and used the pants leg to wild-horse him against those bars."

"That's good, Buck. He can't accuse you of smuggling that rope in to me, then, huh?"

"Right now," Buck said, "one northern Montana sheriff is very mad and very confused. He told me he searched town. Did he search this room?"

"I guess so. He and another fellow came to the hotel, but I hid on top, and then after they left I dropped down the back and used the key you gave me."

"How do you like jail?"

"I don't."

Buck sighed. "You and me have been in too many jails, friend." He thought of beautiful Circle Five. "We should settle down somewhere. Maybe up in Canada, huh?"

"You talk crazy, Buckshot. You'd be wanting to move inside of a month, your pants saddle itchy. What's next?"

"Maybe we should just ride north into Canuck Territory?"

Tortilla Joe eyed his partner. "You're joking. You have to be. They burned Wad down. Maybe somebody sneaked in and murdered him, a defenseless man with a broken leg."

"You talk a good case, Tortilla. Maybe the wrong one's pretending to be a lawyer?"

"They beat you up," Tortilla Joe said. "They buffaloed you cold twice. Look at your face. Black eye, lip split, bruises. And you say to pull out? Do I hear right?"

"There's nothing wrong with your ears," Buck said, "but somehow I don't think Wad was the guy we used to know."

"He changed. We all change. But he broke us out of jail, remember? And somebody murdered him."

"Why?"

"I don't know. I was here free but a short time, and then the fight and the fire and I'm in jail."

"I've learned quite a bit about Wad. He was the only farmer who'd been a cowboy. The others have been farmers back East all their lives. Wad used to drink occasionally with Rocky Pincus and Circle Five, one farmer told me."

"That I don't believe, Buckshot."

"What makes you say that?"

"When I was with Wad he cursed Rocky Pincus and Circle Five. He said Pincus played up to his wife before she left."

"I heard that, too," Buck admitted. "But I still claim somebody sneaked in and killed Wad to keep him from talking. They got scared when I came into town pretending to be a lawyer. They got scared Wad might tell me something, so they sneaked in and murdered him."

"Who?"

"I haven't got the slightest idea," Buck said. "What would Wad have to tell you?"

"I don't know that, either. But I do know that Wad had been shooting something into himself with a hypodermic needle." He mentioned the needle marks on the arms of Wad Matthews and Old Man Twiggs. "I wonder how Wad got along with this druggist?"

"Ah, the lovely redheaded Marcia Andrews, huh? I don't know. He never mentioned her. I never saw the needle marks. I remember now, the short while I was around him, he always wore long-sleeved shirts, even on the hottest afternoon."

"This lovely redhead—as you call her—shoots something into Old Man Twiggs. And this something —whatever it is—might be what makes him act and talk so loco."

Tortilla Joe frowned. "You made me remember something. Once or twice when I was with Wad waiting for you to come, Wad talked sorta crazy, too."

"Like how?"

"Oh, he talked about how rich he was going to be soon, and I said no farmer ever got rich farming, and he winked at me and acted kind of—how do you say it in English?"

"Acted kind of sly?"

"Yeah, that's the word. Like he had a secret. And like he was a little bit drunk, but he never had whiskey on his breath. I thought maybe he'd had a bottle hidden, but he never stunk of booze. I didn't understand it."

Buckshot McKee walked up and down the small room, eyes narrowed in thought. Finally he stopped in front of Tortilla Joe, who looked up at him with a question in his dark eyes.

"Okay, pal," Buck said, "we've been talking, and we've been going round and round, but we still haven't hit anything solid yet. Why did Circle Five jump on Wad and no other farmer? Mrs. Twiggs told me she'd left orders for Circle Five not to touch the farmers. Yet they wiped out Wad, and a man got killed while they did it."

"I don't know, Buckshot."

Suddenly Buck froze. Boots came up the stairway and turned in the direction of Buck's room. Tortilla Joe had his hand on his holstered gun, his dark head cocked as he listened. Buck stood poised, coat-tail back, his hand also on his leathered pistol.

The boots stopped in front of Buck's door, stood there a long moment, and then a man mumbled drunkenly, "Hell, I made the wrong turn when I left the stairs."

The boots left. Later, a door opened, slammed closed, and then silence settled again.

"Neither do *I* know," Buck continued, "but Pincus had a reason—and a good one—for wiping out Matthews. I figure Pincus aimed to kill Wad Matthews in that raid, but didn't get the chance. Tell me all about it."

Circle Five raiders had hit early in the afternoon. They had fired the barn and imprisoned Tortilla Joe and Wadsworth Matthews in the house, where the two had fought shooting from doors and windows.

"Circle Five hid out in the rocks. Whitey Jordan made a mistake. He stood up. Wad pulled down on him with a rifle. Whitey fell dead, shot through the heart."

"You sure Wad killed Whitey?"

Tortilla Joe looked at his lanky partner. "Wad shot right at him. Who else but Wad would have shot him?"

"Whitey and his brother, Blacky, fought all the time," Buck said. "Cain killed Abel. Brothers today kill each other, too. I've heard that Whitey and Wad were rather close friends."

"I didn't know that. Blacky could have shot his brother. But it looked to me like Wad plugged Whitey. Anyway, the murder charge was filed against me and Wad, remember?"

"And still is against you," Buck pointed out.

Tortilla Joe grimaced. "Well, the farmers heard the shooting, and one came into town fast. He told Sheriff Jenkins that if the sheriff didn't stop the fight at Matthews's farm, he and the other farmers would get rifles and pistols and join in on Wad's side."

"So Jenkins stopped it?"

"He deputized some men and rode out with that deputy, Watson. But by that time, it was all over. Pincus claimed me and Wad had started it, that he and his Circle Five men rode in for a drink of water and we just opened up on them. But he fired first."

"And Pincus swore out a warrant charging you and Matthews with murder, huh?"

"That's the deal, Buck."

Buck continued pacing, hands behind his back under his coattail. "I wish I knew where Wad's wife was," he said. "She could tell plenty."

"Wad told me she went to Malta, Buck."

"Oh, he told me nothing of the sort."

"He said she was still there, working in a cafe. She might know something, at that."

Buck walked to the window. He looked down on Yellowstone City's dirty, dusty main street. Dusk was creeping in, but there would be the usual long Montana summer twilight native to these far north ranges. He rubbed his jaw thoughtfully.

"You ride to Malta," he said, "and talk with her, if you can find her. On my horse."

"When?"

"When it gets dark. You can sneak in the back door of the livery stable. I'll be talking to the hostler in the front of the barn. You can easily steal my horse."

"Why steal your horse? Why not steal somebody else's cayuse? As long as I have to have a horse-stealing charge over me, too, why steal yours?"

"Because you know I'd never prosecute you if you happened to be caught. They hang horse thieves in this section, you know."

Tortilla Joe patted his thick dark-skinned neck. "They also hang murderers," he pointed out. "And therefore I'll make sure I'm not caught."

"Unless the hostler sees that my horse is gone, I'll report the loss tomorrow morning to the sheriff. That'll give you a good many hours to get out of the country."

"Where'll I meet you at when I come back? It's risky riding into town."

"Mind that north of town about two miles is a high flat-topped butte? We meet on the other side of that."

"When?"

Buck paused, considering. "I'll ride out there three days from now and check."

"Make it two days. You've got a fast bronc."

"I'll buy some grub at the Merc. You can tote some in my saddlebags. You hungry?"

"They didn't feed good at the jail. They fed me bread—like you *Americanos* eat. I'm hungry for a mess of good old Mexican *tortillas, amigo.*"

Buck smiled. "I'll buy you some cornmeal flour. You can make some *tortillas* on the trail. You can't pound them out with your hands in this room. Everybody in the hotel would hear you."

"Bullets?"

"My rifle's on my saddle. Loaded except for the barrel, and there's .30-30 and .45 cartridges in the saddlebags."

"I sleep now. You go buy the grub. The bed in the

jail is made of rocks. What's the name of Wad's wife?"

"Delphia, he told me."

"Long and tough name. I like simple names for my women—Maria, Alicia, Soledad, Guadalupe. Lupe for short, huh?"

"I'll lock the door from the outside," Buck said.

Finally twilight died and night came. Tortilla Joe, gunnysack half full of groceries, went down the back stairway into the deserted alley twenty minutes after Buck had left with a bottle in his hip pocket for the livery barn hostler.

Buck and the hostler sat in front of the barn, taking nips from the bottle. The hostler apparently didn't notice that this new lawyer, although he often raised the quart bottle, didn't lower the bottle's line a bit.

By eleven, the hostler was sleeping in front of his barn, the almost empty bottle under his snoring body. He was there for the night.

Buck walked back into the barn, smelling hay and manure and sweat and riding gear. His sorrel gelding was gone. So were his saddle, bridle, rifle, and saddlebags, but his warbag had been left behind, and Buck left it where it was.

He went out the wide front door. He toed the hostler slightly, the body limp under his boot, and he grinned as he went to his hotel room and to bed.

The next forenoon, he again checked at the barn. The hostler was nowhere around. The barn held a few horses, most of them with Circle Five brands, all unsaddled—evidently spare horses for Circle Five riders.

Buck left by the rear door. He heard snoring. The

hostler had evidently got too hot in the sun. He had crawled into the shade of the buckbrush.

He slept soundly, bottle in his right hand. Buck saw that the bottle was empty. An idea hit the lanky Texan.

He had planned to report the loss of his horse to the sheriff's office, but now he thought better of it. He would just keep the hostler so drunk that he would never miss the sorrel gelding.

This would require another quart of bourbon. Buck grinned and hurried toward the saloon.

"One quart," the bartender of the Broken Cinch said. "One quart coming up."

"And then *going* down," Buck said.

Chapter Ten

ALTHOUGH he had never before hunted a man, Deputy Sheriff Isaac Watson prided himself on being a man hunter, his information gained by reading Wild West stories.

Sheriff Jenkins was sure the Mexican had gone south and had got a horse from either one of the farmers or Circle Five; but no farmer reported a horse missing, and Circle Five had lost no saddler, either.

Deputy Watson claimed the Mexican had gone

north, heading for the Canadian border. He did this because he wanted to be contrary to his boss.

Thus the deputy stationed himself between Tortilla Joe and the cow town of Malta on that moon-filled Montana August night, and Tortilla Joe, an old hand at dodging the law, saw the deputy without Watson even being aware that he was watched.

Tortilla Joe rode ridges, watching the moonlit land below. Deputy Sheriff Watson rode low areas, scanning the skyline, as it was done in dime novels.

It is easier to look down than to look up, and a man on the ridges can see more clearly what is below than the man in the flats can see what is above. Thus Tortilla Joe spotted Deputy Sheriff Isaac Watson easily.

And Tortilla Joe frowned first, then smiled.

He didn't hate the blustering deputy. To him, Deputy Isaac Watson was a man who was doing a job he was hired for, nothing else. But Tortilla Joe had little if any respect for the lawman's intelligence.

Watson rode at a walk on a trail running through occasional groves of big cottonwood trees. He rode east. Tortilla Joe was west and south of the deputy.

Tortilla Joe remembered all the boasting this arrogant but ignorant man had made outside of his cell. He had been forced to sit in the cell on his hard bunk and listen to Deputy Watson spout off his big mouth.

Tortilla Joe and his horse were hidden in a black clump of igneous boulders. Deputy Watson hadn't the least idea that a living soul was within miles of this wilderness.

Tortilla Joe dismounted, ground-tied Buck's sorrel, took Buck's lasso from the saddle's fork, and went downhill, keeping hidden in the brush and behind boulders. Soon he came to the trail along which Deputy Watson would ride.

The Mexican's first thought was to tie the rope about two feet high across the trail between two big trees. Thus he would trip Watson's bronc and send Watson and horse flying. He decided against this. He might hurt the horse, and he had no desire to inflict pain on a blameless animal.

He decided to tie the rope just high enough so it would catch the deputy around the middle and snap him from his horse. This was easily done, and Tortilla Joe stepped back, realizing that in the fickle moonlight he had to look hard to see the rope.

Anybody galloping along, not knowing a rope was ahead, would never see it.

The Mexican now knelt and put his right ear against the ground, thus picking up the vibrations of the deputy's approaching saddle horse, a trick his Yaqui Indian relatives had taught him when he had been a mere child in the state of Sonora, Old Mexico.

He judged horse and rider to be about three hundred yards away, and he wanted them closer. Accordingly, he waited patiently, smiling slightly as the horse neared, and when the bronc was about fifty yards away, the Mexican hurriedly backtracked about fifty feet up-trail, the rope between him and Deputy Isaac Watson.

Tortilla Joe knelt, hidden; he cleared his throat. Then he screamed in a high-pitched voice, "My leg— my horse—he fell—my leg—it's brok—"

There was a moment of silence, and then came Deputy Watson's bellowing voice, "Who is it?"

"Me—my leg—"

"I'm coming," the deputy said.

Again Tortilla Joe's ear sought the ground. When he judged man and horse were close to the rope, the Mexican looked up—and just in time.

Watson came at a hard gallop. The rope caught him just above the gun belt, his horse at a dead run. The horse thundered on, but Watson wasn't on him.

Watson grunted, then stopped. The rope sagged out like the string on an archer's bow. For one long moment, the rope reached its outer limits. Watson was hung against space, bronc running out from under him.

Then the rope snapped back. Watson shot backward like an arrow. With a wild yelp, he smashed into a small box elder tree. Tortilla Joe heard the breaking of limbs. Leaves fell, and Watson fell with them.

Watson crashed down on his back. He didn't move. Tortilla Joe let Watson's terrified bronc lope madly by, empty stirrups flapping.

Tortilla Joe stared. He had expected to wreak some havoc, but not this much. Watson had hit the rope with terrible force. Tortilla Joe hoped the lawman had not been killed.

He circled and came in behind Watson, who still lay prone. Tortilla Joe squatted beside the deputy. He put his thumb and forefinger on Watson's windpipe and felt the man's heartbeat, solid and true.

Watson had banged his head against the box elder.

He had knocked himself unconscious. Tortilla Joe doubted if Watson would know what had happened when the deputy came to.

Tortilla Joe put Watson's big hands on Watson's chest. In his right hand he put a sprig of box elder leaves. He then untied his rope. He found Watson's horse down-trail a hundred feet. The horse had stepped on his nigh rein, had got the leather tangled around his hock, and had stopped.

Tortilla Joe hurriedly unsaddled the horse and laid the saddle and wet blanket on the trail. He then slipped the bridle from the horse, thus freeing the beast.

He slapped the horse on the rump. The horse wheeled and galloped madly away, glad to be free of rider, saddle, and bridle. The Mexican then lay the bridle over the saddle and the blanket.

Deputy Sheriff Watson was now afoot. Tortilla Joe figured that the closest house was that of one of the farmers, about seven miles away.

High-heeled riding boots were not made for walking, Tortilla Joe well knew. By the time Deputy Isaac Watson reached the farmer's holdings, the lawman's heels would sport nice calluses.

The saddle would be too heavy to carry such a distance, Tortilla Joe figured. That would necessitate another trip to this area for the blowhard deputy.

Tortilla Joe climbed the hill to his awaiting bronc. Buck's cayuse was fresh from a two-day rest, and noon of the next day found Tortilla Joe riding into the old cow town of Malta, the whistle of a Great Northern freight train in his ears.

He had never been in this town before. He knew that no telephone or telegraph line ran from Yellowstone City, which was inland, to this railroad town. Therefore, Malta would not know that a Mexican had broken jail in faraway Yellowstone City.

He went first to the Malta *Independent,* where he said he was an uncle to a woman named Delphia Matthews, and that he had heard Mrs. Matthews was located in Malta. He discovered that Mrs. Matthews waited table in the Sugar Bowl, for the *Independent*'s editor was a real newspaperman, knowing just about every person in his bailiwick.

Adelphia Matthews was now Adelphia Westrum, he discovered. She had immediately divorced Wad upon arriving in Malta and had just as rapidly married the owner of the Sugar Bowl.

"I don't want to talk about Mr. Matthews," she said, and then Tortilla Joe told her that Wad Matthews was dead. She softened somewhat. "One should have respect for the dead. You say the poor man committed suicide?"

Tortilla Joe nodded.

"I knew he'd come to a violent end," the pretty woman sighed. "What else can I tell you?"

"Did you ever hear your ex-husband mention me or Buckshot McKee?"

"Many times, Mr. Tortilla."

"Wad changed a lot after coming to Montana."

"Oh, did he—and how! He came to Yellowstone City to ride for Circle Five. He'd met Rocky Pincus when he lived in South Dakota, right after we got married. Rocky had trailed some cattle down to Omaha, and he offered Wad a job on Circle Five."

Tortilla Joe listened. The woman's story differed from what Wad had told him. Which one had told the truth?

"But after we got to Yellowstone City, he decided to homestead. Rocky got mad at him. Suddenly Wad changed. He grew thin, cranky, and mean. We didn't share the same—well, bedroom."

"What caused this change?"

"I really don't know, Mr. Tortilla. By this time, Wad and me were poles apart. We argued every word. We snapped and bickered. We just lived in the same house, that's all."

"Did he spend much time away from home?"

"I don't know. I think he made night rides, because a couple of mornings I noticed his saddle horse would be sweaty and tired, but where he went—and what he did—I don't know."

Tortilla Joe realized he was learning exactly nothing. His long ride had, to all intents and purposes, been wasted. "Can you think of anything about your husband's behavior that especially puzzled you, Mrs. Westrum?"

The woman scowled, her fingers playing with a toothpick. "Yes, I believe I remember one odd thing."

One night she had heard an animal sniffing around outside her bedroom window. She had heard rabid coyotes were on the range, and she was afraid. She went to her husband's room.

Her husband's bed was empty. Hesitantly, she

looked out the window. A pet badger was digging a hole. Her fear passed, but her curiosity increased.

"It was after three in the morning, Mr. Tortilla. Where could Wad be at that hour? Everything in town would be closed. I lay awake, waiting. He came in just at dawn."

She had expected Wad to go to bed. Instead, he had gone to the tool shed and got a shovel.

"I watched out the window. What in heaven's name was he doing with a spade at that time of the morning? He carried a small gunnysack, I noticed. It had something in one corner. It must have been heavy, judging from the way the sack hung."

Wad had gone in the direction of the horse corral. The blacksmith shop had cut off her view. She didn't dare sneak outside to see what her husband was doing.

"I wasn't much interested, either. I'd already made up my mind to leave, and I was saving from my household money. He was gone about fifteen minutes. When he came back, he had only the shovel. He put it in the shed and went to bed."

"What do you suppose the sack held?"

"I don't know. But someday, if possible, I'm going back and I'm digging up that corral!"

"You mean, he might have buried money?"

"What else would it be, Mr. Tortilla?"

Tortilla Joe scowled darkly. "Where would he get the money?"

"I don't know. He didn't make much farming, but he always had some money."

Tortilla Joe nodded, deep in thought. He decided

he could learn no more from the present Mrs. Westrum. He ate a big T-bone steak and napped in the livery barn's haymow until dusk, for he wanted to cover most of the trail back in the cool of the night.

When he came down from the haymow, he was surprised to see a gray horse bearing a Circle Five brand in a stall. The hostler told him the horse had been ridden in by a slim blond-haired rider.

Tortilla Joe's first thought was that Circle Five had trailed him into Malta, but common sense made him discard this. He knew that occasionally Circle Five men made the long ride to Malta to celebrate in the saloons along the river.

He remembered that Buck had knocked out a blond youth, one Blacky Jordan, in the Broken Cinch, after Blacky had first sent Buck into dreamland. He also remembered that Buck had been knocked out beside the Antlers Cafe, and had awakened with a brown wrapping-paper note telling him to get out of Yellowstone City and stay out.

Tortilla Joe grinned mischieviously. He borrowed a piece of brown wrapping paper from a store. On it he printed in big block letters: GET OUT OF TOWN AND STAY OUT!

Now all he had to do was to find the Circle Five man and deliver the note. He found the man an hour later as he stumbled, half drunk, from one saloon to the other.

Tortilla Joe immediately identified Blacky Jordan. He came in behind the Circle Five man on silent boots, gun raised.

The .45 hissed down and landed. Blacky Jordan's knees folded, and he lay motionless on his belly.

Tortilla Joe pulled back into the shadows. He looked about, but saw nobody moving. Nobody had seen him slug down this arrogant Circle Five rider.

Grinning, he put the note in Blacky Jordan's breast pocket. Still grinning, he rode out of Malta.

Chapter Eleven

BUCK McKEE sat in Sheriff Jenkins's office the next morning. The sheriff was out in the hills, trying to cut a sign of the Mexican. Deputy Sheriff Watson walked to the water pail. Buck noticed that the deputy limped.

"What's the matter?" Buck asked.

"Got calluses on my heels. Both heels."

Buck frowned. "What happened?"

"Bought new boots. They were too tight. Just walked a block and they raised blisters. No, not these boots, shyster. These are my old comfortable boots."

"You walk kind of bent over," Buck said, "like somebody's just hit you in the belly."

"My gut's acting up. Somethin' I et, I guess. My liver's been bad since I was a kid."

At that moment a Circle Five cowboy rode into sight, leading an unsaddled horse that Buck knew belonged to Deputy Sheriff Isaac Watson.

"What's your horse doing running around loose on Circle Five range?" the cowboy asked.

The deputy shrugged. "Must've busted out of the pasture last night. He's rough on fences. Even rubs open barbwire gates."

"He sure grazed a long ways out to be gone only overnight," the Circle Five man said. "Rocky Pincus run across him six miles north of the home ranch house."

"He has always been a drifter," Deputy Watson said. "Throw him in my night pasture, huh, Clem?"

"Okay, Isaac."

The cowboy rode on, leading Watson's horse. Buck said, "He didn't even say hello to me. I might as well not have been here."

"He's Circle Five," Watson pointed out. "An' Circle Five don't like you. Can you blame them? Knocking both Blacky Jordan and Rocky Pincus cold at one time?"

"That's right," Buck said.

"Nobody around town likes you," the deputy grumbled. "Just this morning I heard Marcia Andrews say to Mrs. Smith that she wished you'd leave town."

"Who said she wished I'd leave town? Mrs. Smith or Marcia Andrews?"

"Can't you understand English? Marcia said she wished you'd pull stakes."

Buck shifted, and dug into his pocket for a match. "I don't understand Miss Andrews. I've never done anything bad to her."

"Well, that's what she said."

A farmer drove up in a spring wagon pulled by a team of chunky matched grays. He had a saddle and a saddle blanket and a bridle in the back of the rig.

"Here's your outfit, Deputy. I found it in the brush just about where you said it might be, when you legged into my cabin this morning."

Buck noticed that the deputy went slightly red, then soon recovered his composure. "Thanks, friend. Just dump it off at my barn, huh?"

The farmer spoke to Buck. "You got an office yet, Lawyer McKee?"

"Not yet," Buck said.

"When you get one, I got some legal work I'd like you to do, but it ain't pressin'."

The farmer drove away.

"I don't understand this," Buck said. "You got hoof calluses. You walk like a mule's kicked you in the midriff. One guy brings in your horse, another your saddle."

"What're you doing in town?" the deputy asked. "You've got no clients here, remember?"

"One was murdered," Buck said.

"Murdered! What the heck you talkin' about? The jury said he kilt himself. Such loose talk'll get you in trouble, shyster!"

"Thanks for the good advice," Buck said, "but if you catch the Mexican, he'll still need my legal services. So I guess I'll just sit around and wait."

"You don't need to wait in this office," Deputy Watson said pointedly. "This ain't no place to loaf. You keep loafin' here, an' I'll have reason to jug you."

"On what charge?"

"Loafin' an' loiterin' on public property. I'll throw you in and toss the key into Milk River."

Buck got to his feet. "I've changed my mind about you and Sheriff Jenkins," he said slowly. "When I first met you, I figured you also drew wages from Circle Five. Now I think you draw wages only from the county. You're both too stupid to commit a bit of larceny on the side."

Deputy Watson got to his feet, fists clenched. "Mister," he gritted, "you're accusin' two honest law officers of traffickin' outside their office. I can jug you for that!"

"I never accused you. I just said you were too stupid to be crooked!"

Deputy Watson moved slowly toward Buck, boots shuffling, fists solid rocks. Just then, Marcia Andrews happened to pass by the open door on the plank sidewalk, and Buck called to her.

"Miss Andrews, please enter. The deputy sheriff is about to assault me. I want you to witness that my hands are wide open and my right hand is far from my gun."

Watson stopped, whirled, and said, "Good morning, Miss Marcia," and then to Buck he hissed, "McKee, get out of here, and fast!"

"With pleasure," Buck said, and left.

He fell into step beside Marcia Andrews, who was going toward her drugstore.

"And did your ride yesterday to Circle Five bring about the results you sought, Mr. McKee?"

"It did."

"And what, may I ask, was the mission concerned with?"

"I wanted Mr. Twiggs to drop charges against my client, the Mexican, but that he wouldn't do. He seems in very poor physical condition, Miss Andrews. Were somebody to ask me, I'd say you are a rather incompetent doctor."

Anger touched her cheeks momentarily. "Nobody has asked you," she said stiffly, and wheeled into her drugstore with, "*Good-bye,* Mr. McKee."

Buck lifted his hat sardonically. "*Good-bye,* Miss Marcia." He continued on to the Broken Cinch, where he bought a quart of bourbon in the saloon, deserted except for the bartender.

"No customers?" Buck asked.

"Too early. Looks like the Mex got away for good, huh?"

"I hope not," Buck said. "I need him as a client, even if he hasn't any money. A lawyer without a client isn't much of a lawyer in my estimation. Sheriff Jenkins will catch him. I have faith in the sheriff."

"I'm glad to hear that," the bartender said. "You're the only one in town that has faith, it seems, in our estimable sheriff. You drink rather hard, huh?"

"Is that your business?"

"That makes two quarts in less than a day. You carry your liquor well, sir."

Buck put the bottle in his pocket. "Thanks."

He went down the street to the livery barn, went through the barn—noticing his sorrel was still gone —and came to a small log cabin where the hostler lived. The door was open. Buck entered without knocking. The hostler lay on a filthy bunk, mouth gaping open as he slept in a drunken bliss.

Buck placed the bottle beside the man's outflung hand and left. He would not report his missing sorrel to the sheriff's office. With the hostler drunk and not minding his stable, nobody would miss the sorrel. He would keep the hostler saturated, too.

He squatted in front of the stable, looking at the ugly heat-drenched town, wishing that he knew what Wad Matthews had known. They would bury Wad in the morning. He was in the lumberyard's back office now, in a homemade pine box.

Sheriff Jenkins rode in on a wind-blowing, sweaty buckskin, nodded at Buck, then rode into the barn. Buck followed. "Any luck?" Buck asked.

"Found me some boot marks about ten miles straight south in a sand wash," the sheriff said, stripping his saddle from his tired horse. "Bronc played out on me, though, so I headed back for a fresh horse an' Injun Joe."

"Injun Joe?"

"Yeah, an ol' Sioux buck here. Can track a wildcat acrost water. Rode with Custer. We'll head out again soon. Where's your bronc?"

"He needed fresh grass. Been eating too much dry hay lately. So I picketed him out in the brush along the river."

"Good for a horse to get a change of pasture." The sheriff looked about. "Where's the hostler?"

"Drunk. Out in his cabin. Can't move. I'll rack your horse. You look spent. Get something cold from the Broken Cinch to wash the alkali from your gullet."

"You're a real man, McKee. I thank you."

Sheriff Jenkins bowlegged out, swollen with his own importance. Buck wadded bluejoint hay and carefully wiped down the buckskin after watering the gelding at the tank.

He tied the horse in a stall and went upstairs and shoveled down hay from the mow into the horse's manger. When he climbed down the ladder, he noticed Louise Twiggs riding down the main street toward the barn.

He stood there and admired her blonde beauty, thinking how lucky Old Man Twiggs was, and how unfortunate the Old Man was also. Mrs. Twiggs rode an ornate Miles City sidesaddle. Buck helped her to the ground, catching a whiff of her nice perfume. She pulled her gauntlets from her small hands.

"You work here now, Mr. McKee?"

"The hostler's on a drunk," Buck explained. "And this also helps me pass the time. Unless the sheriff catches the Mexican, I'm an attorney presently without a client."

"Sheriff Jenkins dropped in on Circle Five last night and asked for somebody to ride to Malta to send word along the Great Northern wires that the Mexican had escaped."

"Who went?"

"Your bosom friend, Blacky Jordan."

Buck gave this information a moment's thought. Blacky Jordan might see Tortilla Joe in Malta.

Louise Twiggs seemed very nervous. She kept twisting a blue silk handkerchief.

"How's your husband?"

"No better, Mr. McKee. I rode into town for Marcia to ride out and give him an injection."

"Did you ever think of taking him away from here? Moving him into Malta or Havre for medical care?"

She bit her lip. "Yes, I have, but—" Without another word, she walked away.

Buck slept fitfully until dawn, when somebody rapped lightly on his door. "The sky is blue," Buck whispered against the panel, and a husky voice whispered back, "No, it's black," and a saddle-weary Tortilla Joe slid into the room.

"The hostler see you ride in?" Buck asked.

"He was dead drunk in his shack. I rubbed your horse down good. Nobody'd think he'd been ridden all night."

"What'd you find out?"

Tortilla Joe told about ambushing Deputy Sheriff Isaac Watson.

"So that's why he's got foot calluses and walks like a mule's belted him—and why a cowboy came in with his loose horse, and a farmer came in with his saddle. You sure he never recognized your voice when you called for help?"

"I made my voice high—like a woman's," Tortilla Joe said, and then related his brief conversation with the former Mrs. Wadsworth Matthews. "Pincus and Wad met before back East. After Wad got here, he began to be money crazy, the woman said. She was sure he buried money in his corral."

"Where would he get the dough?"

Tortilla Joe shrugged. "She didn't know. She wasn't even sure he buried money."

"Not much to go on," Buck said. "Continue."

Tortilla Joe told about slugging Blacky Jordan and leaving a note with the unconscious Circle Five rider.

"He went to town on Sheriff Jenkins's orders, to send telegrams up and down the Great Northern wires. Mrs. Twiggs told me that. You sure he never saw you?"

"He never saw me, Buckshot. Somebody is coming!"

Boots sounded in the hall, coming toward Buck's door. Tortilla Joe was afoot, hand on his gun. Unless he went out the window, he was trapped—and he didn't have time to swing out the window and climb onto the roof.

Hard knuckles hammered Buck's door. Buck opened the door slightly, with Tortilla Joe hidden behind the door, his back to the wall.

Sheriff Jenkins and an old Indian stood in the hallway, the sheriff carrying a rifle. The Indian was empty-handed.

"This here's Injun Joe," Sheriff Jenkins said. "Him an' me's goin' out to track down the Mex. Noticed your bronc is back in the barn. You just leave him there, McKee."

"You don't want me to leave town?"

"I've thought this over. Seems damn odd that the Mex had somethin' to hang me aroun' the neck with an' escape."

"Is that an accusation, Sheriff?" Buck made his

voice hard. "Sure, I visited my client in his cell. But you searched me when I went to visit him, and I feel sure you searched him and his cell after my visit."

"You just stay in the city limits until I get back," Sheriff Jenkins said and left, Injun Joe dutifully following him.

Buck shut the door. Tortilla Joe holstered his .45. "That was a close one," the Mexican murmured.

Buck could only nod.

Chapter Twelve

ROCKY PINCUS came out of the Circle Five cookshack with six eggs and half a pound of bacon under his gun belt. He scratched his belly and looked at the rising sun. The day, he thought, will be another scorcher.

Spurs chiming, he stalked to the corral, where the night wrangler had just run in the remuda. The saddle horses were still circling inside the pine-pole corral, their shod hoofs kicking up dust.

Circle Five horses were grain fed and rock hard. Circle Five riders rode the best horseflesh in northern Montana. While his hands gathered around him, Rocky Pincus snapped out the day's orders.

Some hands would ride bog holes. Others would turn back stock that tended to drift too far from water. Cowboys roped broncs, threw on saddles, a few horses bucked, and men thundered out to go about the day's chores, until only Blacky Jordan stood with Circle Five's range boss.

"Sent them all ridin' south range," the big blond youth said. "That means you and me scout north range, huh?"

"Sometimes you can even think," Rocky said cynically.

Blacky Jordan's lips tightened, but he said nothing. His head still pounded from the two pistol whippings he had received in the last few days. He had come in last night after the long ride back from Malta.

He had told nobody about being slugged in Malta. He had been found lying unconscious by the town marshal, who had taken him to jail as a drunk, and only when the doctor had examined him was he released.

He had talked to the former Mrs. Wad Matthews, who had told him she had talked a few hours before with a Mexican who called himself Tortilla, or something like that.

Blacky Jordan could add. Two and two made four. Tortilla Joe had headed north for safety in Canada. The Mexican had seen him, Blacky Jordan, ride into Malta, and Tortilla Joe had slugged him cold. But why?

Cold fear gnawed at Blacky Jordan's black soul. He remembered the wild fight at the Matthews farm. Wad Matthews had thrown down on Whitey Jordan at the same time that he had leveled his pistol at Whitey Jordan's heart.

Wad Matthews's bullet had come too late. Blacky

Jordan's bullet, by that time, had torn out the heart of Blacky Jordan's brother.

When the fight had started, Blacky hadn't intended to kill his brother, but he and Whitey had had a vicious quarrel that morning—an argument out in the brush that had led them almost to gunfire. And suddenly, seeing a chance to kill his brother, Blacky Jordan—without thinking—had turned his pistol and shot his brother through the heart.

Had any of the embattled Circle Five gunmen storming Wad Matthews's farmstead seen him shoot his brother? He was sure of all the Circle Five except possibly Rocky Pincus, who had lain behind a boulder not more than two feet away when Blacky had fired the fatal shot.

Ever since the fight, that shot had haunted Blacky Jordan. He had killed his brother. He was doomed to eternal damnation. He had bowed to a sudden whim. And now he would pay for this weakness all his life.

Why had he been so weak?

Now the blond youth looked at Rocky Pincus and quietly asked, "We ready to move another stolen herd soon?"

"Not so damn loud!"

"Rocky, the closest person is Mrs. Twiggs, in the house. Your nerves are jumpy, friend."

"When did I become your *friend?*"

Anger rimmed Blacky Jordan's low words. "Don't get personal. We both got enough on each other to hang the other."

Blacky was feeling out Rocky. Maybe Rocky hadn't seen him murder his brother.

"They don't hang men for stealin' cattle," Rocky Pincus growled. "Jail, yes—but no noose."

Blacky Jordan's spirits lifted. Evidently, Rocky had not seen him, in a moment of blind rage, put the bullet through Whitey's heart.

"Let's not get sidetracked," the blond youth said. "We ride north range together—you and me—to-day?"

"Rope you a good horse," Rocky Pincus growled.

Louise Twiggs watched from the parlor window as the two riders swept out of Circle Five's hoof-hammered yards, riding fast and high on stirrups toward Circle Five's huge northern range.

Louise Twiggs's blue eyes hardened. She wondered how many thousands of acres Circle Five ran cattle over. She judged Circle Five's range to be eighty miles east and west, and about sixty miles deep north and south.

How many thousand head of cattle did Circle Five hold? Last year's beef roundup showed a total of eighteen thousand five hundred and sixteen head of cows, bulls, steers, and calves.

But was the count honest?

Her husband hadn't ridden beef roundup for three years now. Rocky Pincus could be stealing the spread blind, for it was he who ran a tally count on Circle Five stock.

Rocky Pincus had come into Circle Five foreman-ship four years ago, when the old foreman, Matt Carter, was killed when a bronc went over backwards with him, crushing his chest. Since then, everything had apparently gone wrong.

Soon Old Man Twiggs had become bedridden. Farmers had moved in, including Wadsworth Matthews. Now Circle Five—against her wishes—had moved in and burned down Wadsworth Matthews's farm buildings. Why had Rocky Pincus picked on Matthews and not some other farmer?

Matthews had seemingly played the middle of the road, not being aligned with Circle Five or with his fellow farmers. Why hadn't Circle Five burned down the buildings of Hank Slocum, the head farmer, the leader and president of the local Grange?

When one fought an enemy, one hit the top enemies first, didn't one? And so ran the thoughts of the lovely blonde woman standing there at the big window, hidden by the curtain, as she watched Circle Five's arrogant foreman and Blacky Jordan thunder out, heading north onto the limitless sweeps of Circle Five range.

A hopeless feeling surged through her. She seemed alone and desolate—a lost soul without friends, without hope. And then she thought of the tall lawyer, Oliver McKee.

Yesterday in the town livery barn she had almost told McKee of her fears that Pincus was stealing Circle Five cattle, and that Marcia Andrews and Pincus were working hand in hand to keep Old Man Twiggs doped up and dreamy so that their scheme would meet no opposition.

She had also thought of expressing her suspicions to Sheriff Jenkins, but she hadn't because she reasoned that he could and would do nothing. Besides, she doubted if he would give her story any credence.

For what evidence did she have that pointed toward rustling on Circle Five? She had none. She only had suspicions. And the law needed evidence, not supposition.

She went to her husband's room. Marcia Andrews had given him another injection that morning. He lay silent and stared up into space. He did not look at her when she entered. He said, "Good morning, Maggie."

She had learned that Maggie was a girl who had worked in a Texas saloon. He had become friendly with Maggie, evidently. When his mind really wandered, he persisted in calling his wife Maggie.

"Good morning, John."

She sat beside his bed. He still stared up at nothing. "How was business in the saloon last night?" he asked.

"Rushing," she said.

He said, "Good," and his eyelids fluttered shut. His eyelids were thin and transparent. She felt a great fear clutch at her heart. The fear was that he would soon be dead. Then she would be completely alone. . . .

She grabbed his scrawny hand and clutched it to her full bosom, breathing deeply.

"You love me, don't you, now, Maggie?" he asked.

"With all my heart," she said, and thought of the two riders, Rocky Pincus and Blacky Jordan. By this time, they would have crossed Milk River at Miles's Crossing, and should be on the north benchlands, sweeping north.

Pincus and Jordan hit the muddy water on the

dead run, splashing it high. Their broncs had to swim in the middle of the river for about twenty feet.

A good water horse swam high in the water, neck held up and the powerful hoofs paddling, the center of the saddle always dry.

Both men squatted on their saddles now, hanging on to horns, boots close together on the saddle's dry center. Steel-shod front hoofs ground on gravel, and the horses pulled out of the stream, hind quarters dripping water.

Both men fell back into their saddles. The north bank was steep, and a dim trail cut the ridge, a trail made by cattle going down to water. The horses hunched up this path, dirt sliding under them, and came panting up onto the mesa.

The flat ran out about a quarter mile, then lifted into hills, dim and blue, that ran endlessly to the north and east and west, finally dying in the north far across the Canadian border.

They loped the broncs now, two big men riding stirrup to stirrup, men who at heart disliked and possibly hated each other—two men bound together by the one desire: money. And around them, evil and strong, was the aura of thievery, of cattle rustling.

Blacky Jordan leaned close and hollered, "Where do you figger the Mex went, Rocky?"

"I don't know," came back the shouted reply, "but I do know that he'll have a murder charge against him all his life until he's caught."

"You sure he shot my brother?"

Rocky Pincus pulled his horse to a running walk. It was too much to shout over galloping hoofs.

"Don't talk like an idiot, Blacky. You know and I know that Mex never shot Whitey."

Blacky Jordan's heart fell. He tried to make his voice level as he asked, "Then, who did?"

Rocky Pincus swung a hard, questioning glance at the blond youth. "You gone nuts, Blacky? You know who kilt your brother. You seen Wad swing a rifle down and shoot Whitey through the heart, didn't you?"

Blacky Jordan felt years younger. "Okay, the Mex never shot my brother. You had him arrested for killing Whitey. Do you think you could have made it stick in court?"

Rocky Pincus laughed sourly. "With Circle Five hand after hand getting up and testifying he'd seen the Mex shoot your brother? How'd you get so full of loco questions?"

"But what if one of the hands told the truth to the court?"

Rocky Pincus tapped his holstered .45 suggestively. "Another loco question, Blacky. What happened to you down in Malta? Somebody hit you over the coconut again?"

It was a coincidence, nothing more—but still, Blacky Jordan's face reddened.

"I'm going to kill me that Oliver McKee," Blacky growled. "No man coldcocks me an' lives . . ."

"Tie into him," Rocky said. "If you don't, I will. He knocked me into dreamland, too, remember?

"Who the heck could forget?"

Rocky Pincus devoted some thinking to Buck McKee. He tried to remember every bit of conversation he had had with the late Wadsworth Matthews. Had Wad at any time mentioned this Mexican, Tortilla Joe, and this tall man, Oliver McKee?

He couldn't remember Wad ever saying those two names. But yet, somehow, he seemed to get the impression that this Mexican was a friend of Attorney Oliver McKee's.

Yet, that was illogical. What self-respecting lawyer would have a saddle bum for a friend?

Why had the Mexican been at Wad Matthews's farm? Wad had said the Mexican had stopped and asked to stay a few days, saying he would pay for his grub and bunk.

Wad had said the Mex was a stranger to him.

Darn Wad, anyway! Why hadn't the farmer been content with his cut in this rustling operation, and not demanded a greater percentage? If Wad hadn't been so greedy, he would still be alive today.

When Marcia Andrews had introduced Wad Matthews to the needle, Wad had gone downhill fast, and he needed more and more of the drug—with Marcia raising the price higher and higher for each shot.

Wad had even threatened to notify the government authorities that he was a dope addict. And had Uncle Sam's agents moved in, they would have discovered that Old Man Twiggs, too, had been put on dope, and all would have been lost.

"You're almighty serious," Blacky Jordan cut in. "Yonder's a bunch of Circle Five steers, boss."

Rocky Pincus came back to saddle. "Make good beef for the Injuns," he said jokingly.

"Injuns will chew on them sooner or later, huh?

We shove them east in a few nights with the others we got cached out?"

Pincus and five Circle Five cowboys—including Blacky—sold stolen Circle Five stock to an Indian agent on Fort Peck Assiniboine Reservation, some miles to the east where Milk River joined the mighty Missouri.

"Don't rush things," Rocky Pincus growled.

The Circle Five range boss and the blond rider circled the steers, heading them northeast. Pincus rode automatically, his strong body fitted deep between fork and cantle, while his thoughts again ranged far afield.

He had meant to kill Wad Matthews in that fight, but miraculously Wad had come through only wounded. And when this shyster came, this McKee, Wad had become doubly dangerous. What if he had revealed to Lawyer McKee the complete details of this rustling scheme?

Rocky Pincus sighed. In one way, he hated to have had to sneak up the hotel's back stairs, put Wad's pistol to Wad's ear, and then, with Wad dead, fasten the dead man's hand around the gun to make it look like suicide.

He and Wad Matthews had, in one sense, been rather good friends. Now he wondered if anybody had seen him smuggle Wad's gun and gun belt out of Sheriff Jenkins's office.

He was sure nobody had seen him. He had come in when the office had been empty, with Deputy Sheriff Isaac Watson out, and Sheriff Jenkins back talking to the Mexican prisoner.

No, everything was watertight, Rocky Pincus reasoned. But he wondered where Wad Matthews had cached the money he had earned from rustling Circle Five cattle. Wad had cached that gold somewhere, for each raid was paid off in gold . . . and gold only.

But where?

Wad had had quite a stake, too. Must've run around twenty thousand or so, anyway, Rocky Pincus thought.

Then he debated whether perhaps the former Mrs. Matthews knew where Wad had cached his gold. But common sense told Rocky Pincus that had she known, by this time she would have dug up the gold for herself.

Wad Matthews's gold was lost to him, Rocky Pincus reasoned. As he slapped the free end of his catch-rope over a steer's wide rump, his thoughts swung to the lovely Marcia Andrews, and his blood quickened at the memory of the redheaded druggist.

Marcia was demanding a bigger cut in the results of these cattle raids. She threatened to stop supplying dope to Old Man Twiggs unless she was paid more.

Rocky Pincus's heavy brows pulled down. It might be that he would have to get rid of Marcia . . . for once and for always, like he had done with Wadsworth Matthews.

Logic suddenly discarded this plan. Without Marcia's dope, Old Man Twiggs would regain his mentality and strength; he would stop the rustling, here and now. No, Marcia was needed, and needed badly.

Her demands for more money would be met.

Again Rocky Pincus thought of Oliver McKee. Mc-

Kee was not ignorant. McKee might be more than a lawyer. Marcia was ordering a lot of dope lately; the United States dope boys might be suspicious. They might have access to the books of wholesale druggists.

Was McKee a government man, traveling under the disguise of a lawyer? Pincus knew this was possible. He realized again that McKee would have to go.

He looked about the endless land with the huge bowl of blue sky overhead. Miles and miles of sagebrush and greasewood and bluejoint grass stretched in all directions.

A man needed but six feet of land. And here in the tumbling northern wilderness many a six feet of land had never felt the hoof of a horse, the moccasin of a Sioux, or even the split hoof of the now-vanished buffalo.

You could kill a man—and bury him on this prairie —and inside of a few days his grave would be grass-covered, unmarked, never to be found.

Rocky Pincus suddenly remembered McKee buffaloing Blacky Jordan cold. McKee had pulled him by the neckcloth and jerked his head down, and McKee's pistol barrel had also knocked *him,* Rocky Pincus, into dreamland.

Pincus's weather-beaten face reddened.

McKee was a hard, tough man.

Damned tough. . . .

Chapter Thirteen

BUCK MCKEE was no fool. He knew his life was in danger. Rocky Pincus and Circle Five had really no excuse for his being buffaloed cold twice and beaten up. Circle Five wanted him out of this range.

He also realized he could do little if any good hanging around Yellowstone City. He sat in Sheriff Jenkins's office with a dour Deputy Watson at three that afternoon, when the sheriff and Injun Joe returned empty-handed.

Injun rode an old swaybacked pinto mare. He didn't stop at the office but rode on down the street. Sheriff Jenkins dismounted stiffly, hammered dust from his old Stetson, and said, "Danged Injun! He claims he tracked for Custer, too. He couldn't track a turtle across a mud hole."

"No sign of my client, huh?" Buck asked.

"Nary a sign, McKee."

Deputy Watson listened, hands hanging between his legs, eyes on his boss, then on Buck.

Buck got to his feet. "I give up, gentlemen. I'm not establishing an office in Yellowstone City, much as I care to. Things have started out bad. Everything's run against me. One client mur—well, a suicide."

"You almost said murdered," Sheriff Jenkins said,

114

forgetting to wheeze. "The coroner's jury said Matthews had shot hisself, remember?"

Buck was immediately unctious. "I do beg your pardon, Sheriff. I am convinced that the Mexican is guilty. Had he not been guilty, he would not have busted jail. I ask your permission, Sheriff Jenkins, to ride out of Yellowstone City, possibly never to return."

Sheriff Jenkins thumbed his bottom lip in reflection. Buck shot a glance at Deputy Watson. Deputy Watson's eyes had shown a momentary glow.

"Good idea," Watson said.

Buck paid the sour deputy no attention, his eyes on Sheriff Jenkins, who seemingly still debated Buck's question. Buck let time go on. The sheriff would soon render his verdict! He was feeding his ego.

"Promise never to return?" the sheriff wheezed.

"I do," Buck said.

"Okay, how long will it take you to get out of town?"

"As soon as I pack my gear in my hotel room, and saddle my horse."

"I give you thirty minutes." Sheriff Jenkins was all business. Buck thanked him for his cooperation and then stuck out a hand to Deputy Sheriff Watson, who grudgingly got to his feet and grudgingly shook Buck's hard hand with a limp paw.

"Good luck, shyster," Watson said.

Buck went down the main street, boots hammering on the old planks. He looked into the Broken Cinch. The bartender was alone. Buck told the man he was leaving. The bartender insisted they drink to Buck's departure.

"Very sensible thing to do," the bartender said. "You got off on the wrong foot, shyster, and sometimes when a man starts out wrong in a town, he just ain't got no chance."

Buck raised his bourbon. He admitted this was good logic. He asked the bartender to say good-bye for him to Rocky Pincus and Blacky Jordan.

"You have got a good sense of humor!" The man slapped Buck on the back. "Another for the trail, shyster?"

Buck almost winced at the word *shyster*. Soon he would never hear that word again applied to his person.

He also stopped in to say *adios* to Marcia Andrews. The lovely redhead sat on a high stool behind the counter reading a druggist's textbook. Buck saw that the book's title was *Opium and its Derivatives*.

Upon seeing him, Marcia hurriedly put the book down in her lap, hiding the title, but Buck had already glimpsed it. He told her he was going, and he looked at her trim ankles, her right leg swinging idly as she sat, attractive and lovely, on the high stool.

"Why, I hate to see you leave, Mr. McKee."

Buck thought, One of the biggest lies I've ever heard from male or female, and he said he hated to leave, too, but apparently there wasn't enough legal business in Yellowstone City for two attorneys. At this statement, the redhead bobbed her pretty head in agreement.

Buck noticed she wore a long-sleeved blouse. He

couldn't remember her in anything but long sleeves. He thought of the pockmarked arms of the dead Wadsworth Matthews and Old Man Twiggs.

"Reading a novel?" he asked.

"No, studying some pharmacology, Mr. McKee. Good day, sir, and good luck."

Buck was dismissed.

Twenty-seven minutes later, warbag tied behind his saddle, he headed south toward the Matthews farm. The eyes of the townspeople peered openly from the street or from behind curtained windows.

He came to the farm where the heavyset farmer and his wife had been loading their cookstove. He saw smoke from the cabin's chimney, and the farmer's wagon—now empty—stood in front of the shack.

The farmer saw him, and he and his wife and the boys came out to greet him. "Thought you'd left by now," Buck said.

"We changed our minds," the farmer said. "You came and offered to provide legal counsel free to Wad and the Mexican, so we took heart and decided to stay."

Buck's heart fell. He told the farmer he was just riding over to inspect the ruins of the Matthew farm. He couldn't bring himself to tell the man he was leaving.

He circled the ruins of the Matthews farmstead carefully before riding to the burned-down area, for he remembered the first day he had come to Yellowstone City, and how the Circle Five man had been hiding in the ravine to trap him.

Nobody guarded the ruins. He rode to the corral. To his surprise, the area inside the burned-down corral poles had been carefully spaded, the earth raw and turned over.

He dismounted, walked around and kicked clods, then rode up the trail a ways, coming upon a camp at the springs where he had washed and shaved.

The camp appeared deserted. It consisted of a tent and a ring of stones serving as a fireplace. Buck saw two shovels leaning against a cottonwood. Each showed signs of recent use, as each was shiny.

"Hello the camp," he called. "Lawyer Oliver Mc-Kee here on horseback."

The sounds echoed, then died. He had his mouth open to call again when a man came from the brush, rifle in hand. "What's the trouble?" the man asked surlily.

Buck shrugged. "Nothing's the matter, sir. I take it you've been digging in the corral of the lately departed Wad Matthews?"

"Matthews? Who is he?"

Buck heard brush crackle behind him. A woman came out carrying a shotgun. She was shapely in tight-fitting overalls and a man's shirt, and wore men's shoes.

Buck immediately recognized her as the former Mrs. Wadsworth Matthews, for Tortilla Joe had described the woman accurately. He now understood why the corral had been dug up.

"What is this man saying?" the woman asked the man. "That you and I, husband, have been digging up somebody's corral?"

"I don't know what he's talking about!" the man said gruffly. "An' I know darn well he don't know, either!"

Buck lifted his hat. "I'm sorry. The mistake was mine." He turned his horse and rode south.

The ex-Mrs. Wadsworth Matthews and her new husband had returned to the former Mrs. Matthews's home, and had dug for the dead Wad Matthews's reported money.

Buck knew they had found nothing. If they had discovered a cache, they would not be camped by the spring.

Two miles farther on, he left his horse at the base of a hill, with heavy buckbrush hiding the animal. He squatted beside the trail, rifle across his lap, also hidden by the brush.

He didn't have to wait long.

Deputy Sheriff Isaac Watson rode a chunky gray gelding. He rode slowly, leaning from the saddle, eyes searching the trail for a sign of Buck. He rode right past Buck.

Carefully Buck leaned his rifle against a tree, eyes on the deputy's retreating back. Then Buck ran lightly onto the trail. The deputy didn't even hear him.

Buck leaped on the horse's haunches. The startled horse lunged ahead, but by that time, Buck was on Deputy Watson's broad back.

Buck heard Watson ejaculate, "What the—?" and then he had torn the deputy from the saddle. They landed on the ground, Watson on his back, Buck astraddle the deputy, with Buck planting hard rights and lefts on the deputy's wide face.

"Hey, McKee—!"

Buck slammed a right against Watson's nose, a left into the man's mouth, then another right to his left eye. Then he held his other blow back, staring down at Watson in mock horror.

"My Lord," Buck said hollowly, "Deputy Sheriff Isaac Watson—and when I saw you from the back, I thought you were the escaped Mexican, so help me Hanner!"

Buck got off the man hurriedly. He grabbed the stunned deputy's right arm and hauled him to his feet. Then Buck deliberately released him. Watson staggered, lurched, almost fell down, caught his balance, and then leaned against a cottonwood tree, blood trickling from his nose.

"McKee, you gone nuts, man?"

"I was napping in the brush. I heard a horse go by. I only saw your back. And you're a wide man—like the Mexican—"

"You're loco!" Watson snapped.

"Don't call me crazy, Deputy!"

"I'm danged sorry, McKee. I see your point. Yeah, the Mex's broad in the beam—like me—"

Watson's big right boot suddenly lashed out. He aimed to kick Buck's legs out from under him, but Buck leaped and caught the boot. He spilled the deputy hard on the trail, and Watson hit the ground with a solid thud.

The deputy groaned in pain, rolling and holding the small of his back. "No more, no more, lawyer."

Buck said dryly, "I notice you call me *lawyer* now —and not shyster. Why did you trail me?"

"I never trailed you, McKee!"

Buck smiled mercilessly. "I've watched you. You cut my sign and hung on to it."

"I thought mebbe it was the Mex's horse."

"You don't know if the Mexican's mounted or afoot. For all we know, he might be hiding out in Yellowstone City."

"He ain't there. We searched every inch of town. Rocky Pincus sent a rider into town. Rocky claims a Circle Five horse was stole last night. Big black gelding, Rocky says."

Elation speared Buck McKee. Tortilla Joe had sneaked out of Yellowstone City on foot under cover of night. He and Buck had tried to steal a horse out of the town livery, but the hostler had been sober and had been watching his cayuses very faithfully.

Buck would have given his partner his sorrel again, but he needed the horse himself.

"We got a horse-stealin' charge against the Mex now," the deputy said, "an' we hang for that, too, in these here parts."

"Rocky see the Mex steal the horse?"

"No, but who else would steal a horse hereabouts—?"

"Rocky Pincus is a big liar," Buck said. "Before you accuse a man after this, be sure you got the evidence, Deputy."

Watson limped to his feet, and again leaned against the tree. This time, Buck kept beyond the deputy's reach.

"Sheriff Jenkins send you out to trail me?" Buck asked.

"Nah, McKee. It was an error, like I told you—I thought you was the Mex. You've hammered down the law. You've beat up on the legal representative of law and order. I hereby place you under arrest, Oliver McKee!"

"Are you serious?"

"Certainly, I'm serious. My nose is bleedin'. You flattened my lips. My left eye's gonna be black. I arrest you for assault and battery, here and now."

"What do you intend to do with me?"

"Take you to town as my prisoner. Throw you in jail. File legal charges against you. Drag you up for trial when the circuit judge comes to hold court."

"What if I resist arrest?"

"I'll take you in against your will." Deputy Watson noticed Buck had his hand on his holstered gun. His hand likewise dropped down. To his surprise, he found his holster empty. Hurriedly, he looked down on the ground and saw his gun lying about ten feet away.

"How'd my pistol get over there?"

"You lost it when I dragged you from your cayuse," Buck informed him.

Deputy Watson started for his gun. Buck kicked the deputy's boots out from under him. Watson landed on his belly. Buck picked up Watson's .45.

"I don't believe I'll let you arrest me," Buck said, "and it's best you don't have your gun for a while. Your rifle's on your saddle, too. So I'm going to lead your horse down the trail about three miles and turn him loose with your pistol tied to your saddle horn. That okay with you?"

"Hell, no! I get in town and I'll swear out a warrant for your arrest!"

"Who'd serve it?" Buck asked. "You can't, so I guess it'd be up to Sheriff Jenkins, and I doubt if he'd even try."

"I'll see you again!" Watson threatened.

"I hope not, Deputy. You and I never were good friends, you know. Good-bye, sir."

He turned Watson's horse loose in a small valley. Then he squatted on a hill and watched Watson through his field glasses as he hiked along.

The deputy untied his pistol, checked it for loads, found it loaded, and jammed it deep into his greased holster. He swung up onto his horse and looked around for a long, hard moment.

Buck McKee watched with narrowed eyes. For one moment it looked as if the deputy would again take up the trail, since he rode toward Buck for a few hundred feet, eyes glued to the trail.

Then the deputy suddenly reined in. He sat in his saddle for a short time, looking about again.

Buck raised his rifle. He centered the sights on the fork of the deputy's Coggshall saddle.

If Watson rode closer, Buck intended to bury a .30-30 slug in the saddle's fork. He had had a saddle shot out from under him down on the Humboldt River in northern Nevada. The force of the bullet, tearing through leather, rawhide, and wood, had knocked Buck's horse sprawling, so strong had been the blow. Now Buck intended to warn Deputy Watson in a similar manner.

Buck never got the chance. The deputy suddenly turned his bronc, fed him the spurs, and loped back toward Yellowstone City.

Grinning, Buck lowered his Winchester.

Chapter Fourteen

Dusk blanketed northern Montana. Tortilla Joe squatted, and roasted the hind leg of a cottontail rabbit over a small fire hidden back in the boulders.

Buck chewed his rabbit leg. "Not a T-bone steak, *amigo*. Maybe we should forget this mess? Ride north into Canada?"

"They shot my horse dead," Tortilla Joe said. "He was tied in front of Wad's house. I don't know where my saddle is. I had to steal one. They made a horse thief out of me, and they have a murder charge over my head. You joke, huh?"

Buck threw his bone aside. "We don't know if old Wad was right or wrong, angel or sinner. But we do know we owe our lives to him. I couldn't let him lie in a restless grave."

"I agree with you, Buckshot."

Tortilla Joe inspected his rabbit leg. It was burned rather black.

"I never was much of a cook," the Mexican said. "When they jumped Wad on his farm, they beat me up after Wad got wounded, and we had to give up."

Buck McKee twisted a Bull Durham cigarette, cupped the match, extinguished it, and threw it away. "They've treated both of us kind of rough. I got slugged cold twice."

"Who do you figure knocked you cold outside the cafe?"

Buck shrugged. "One of the Circle Five bunch. Pincus, Blacky Jordan—Lord knows who, but Circle Five was behind it, you can bet on that. No, I'm for riding this bronc till he quits pitching—but where do we begin, pal?"

Tortilla Joe sucked a cornhusk cigarette. "You give me your ideas, huh?"

Buck nodded. "This druggist—Marcia Andrews— she's got Old Man Twiggs under dope, the Old Man at first thinking she injected him with some old secret Sioux medicine. Now he's so drugged he doesn't know day from night."

"You say Wad's arm had needle holes, too? That means he used drugs, too, and drugs cost money. Where would he get the money to buy drugs from Marcia?"

"Wad never was on the needle when we knew him before."

"No, I saw his arms many times. Many times we went swimming naked. He had no marks. He got that habit since coming here. Why did he leave South Dakota for Montana? Grass is much better in South Dakota. Winters aren't as hard. Wad was a cowman at heart. A good cowman doesn't move from a good cattle-raising area to one that's not as good."

"Wad met Pincus back East, remember? Pincus got him into this region, I'd say. Pincus offered him money—more than Wad made in South Dakota."

Tortilla Joe nodded. "And then Wad got to taking dope. And maybe he wanted more money from Pincus. And Pincus stormed Wad's house to kill Wad? And Pincus failed, maybe, because I sided Wad with my gun?"

"Yes, and if they killed Wad in cold blood, you could have testified to the murder in court. So they take Wad into town. Then I come along—Pincus is afraid Wad will talk—"

"And Pincus sneaks up the back stairs of the hotel and kills Wad?"

Buck killed his smoke. "That's how I read the sign. How do you read it?"

"This Marcia Andrews—she's in on this, Buck. She's making money, too. Maybe she sneaked in and killed Wad?"

Buck shrugged. "Possibly. But where would this money come from?"

"Cattle. Old Man Twiggs was put out of the way with dope. His wife—she's a woman alone. . . ."

"Rustled stock," Buck said. "Circle Five steers. Where would they go, pal?"

Tortilla Joe rubbed his unshaven jaw. "There's no mining camp within four hundred miles of here, if not farther. Mining camps need lots of beef."

"Closest mines are at Helena, miles and miles away. Closer to five hundred miles, I'd say."

Tortilla Joe looked suddenly at Buckshot McKee, who returned his gaze. "Indian reservation," the Mexican breathed. "East of here, and no more than fifty or so miles, huh?"

"Fort Assiniboine," Buck said.

The partners slept that night on the rimrock, their horses grazing on pickets. Stars sprinkled the deep Montana sky. Tortilla Joe soon snored softly, but Buck McKee, lying on the warm sand with a thin blanket over him, gave himself up to thought as he listened to coyotes yip in the distance.

At dawn, Tortilla Joe pointed his stolen horse and stolen saddle due east. Soon the horse and rider became a dim, dark moving dot against the endless horizon. Buck rode northwest toward the immense Circle Five.

Buck hoped to get Louise Twiggs alone and talk to her. He was sure Old Man Twiggs's blonde wife knew more than she had told him. He was sure cattle were being rustled from Circle Five range. The ranch had no mines or any other source of income.

Maybe Mrs. Twiggs worked in cahoots with the thieves, whoever they were? Maybe her supposedly deep love for her husband was a mere blind?"

Buck scouted from the rimrock a half mile south of the big ranch house, field glasses trained on the spread below. Men came and went on horseback; others moved about the yard.

The bronc-stomper peeled raw Montana cayuses in a corral, taming new horses for the remuda. The big outfit was getting ready for the beef gather.

From the blacksmith shop came the ring of a sledge

on metal. Buck judged that the blacksmith was shrinking the tires on the bed wagon and the cook's rig.

Three waddies were fitting new canvas tops to the two wagons, stretching new white canvas over the hardwood bows.

Louise Twiggs came from the house at two o'clock, sunbonnet covering her blonde hair, long gloves to her wrists, and she watered her flowers along the house and along the rail fence. Buck remembered that Rocky Pincus had crouched in the damp earth outside of Old Man Twiggs's bedroom and had heard every word Louise Twiggs, Old Man Twiggs, and he had said.

Marcia Andrews rode into the ranch at four, two Circle Five riders with her. The Circle Five boys had met her as they had come in from range chores.

She dismounted in front of the stone house. Circle Five led her horse into the barn while she entered the house, black doctor's bag in hand.

Buck considered accosting her if she rode back to Yellowstone City alone, then ruled against it. He had told Sheriff Jenkins he was leaving this range.

He had to work in secrecy. He couldn't reveal to the sheriff, through Marcia Andrews, that he still lurked on Circle Five's range. But he did wish he could rip off one of the woman's sleeves and look at her arms.

About now, he figured, the shrunken veins of Old Man Twiggs would be getting a new shot of Sioux *medicine*.

He saw no more of Mrs. Twiggs that day. Marcia

Andrews left the ranch at dusk, five Circle Five men riding with her back to Yellowstone City.

Buck's glasses spotted Rocky Pincus and Blacky Jordan in the quintet. Evidently, Circle Five rode to town to whet their whistle in the Broken Cinch.

Buck's mouth watered. He had not eaten all day. He imagined a cold Broken Cinch beer trickling down his arid throat. He realized he had to get some grub.

That night, he raided a Circle Five line camp on the south rim of the Circle Five range. To his surprise, the log cabin had a padlock on its door, a clear violation of rangeland etiquette, for invariably a cow-outfit left the doors of its line camps unlocked. Sometimes stray waddies were caught in blizzards or cloudbursts, and needed shelter and grub.

Buck didn't kick in the door. A windowpane was easier to break. He completely cleaned out the line camp of canned goods, and then pitched camp back on a ridge, wondering where Tortilla Joe was and how he was getting along.

Dawn again found him watching Circle Five. Again Louise Twiggs watered flowers, but never left the yard. Rocky Pincus and Blacky Jordan rode into the ranch together at dusk, their horses plodding in weariness.

Buck's powerful glasses showed the pair clearly. Both waddies rode deep between horn and cantle, the way saddle-tired cowboys ride, fitting their bodies to the slow rhythm of their broncs; their broncs were marked by dried sweat, showing they had been ridden hard and fast.

Buck had seen the two leave Circle Five just after Rocky Pincus had issued the day's orders to his men. Pincus and Jordan had crossed Milk River and headed northeast, riding at a long trail-lope. Pincus had been astraddle a chunky mouse-colored buckskin. Blacky Jordan had his kak on a long-legged bay.

Rocky Pincus now was astraddle a blue roan, and Blacky Jordan rode in on a dirty-gray bronc. Somewhere that day, the two had changed mounts at some line camp.

Buck McKee scowled. Why had the two waddies changed horses? Had they encountered some hard riding and played out their original mounts and run in new broncs off the range?

Next forenoon at eleven, Louise Twiggs rode alone toward Yellowstone City, with Buck accosting her in the high cottonwood trees along Beaver Creek.

The blonde's blue eyes narrowed. "I thought you'd left this range, Mr. McKee?"

Her voice was cold. She held her sorrel with hard reins, one leg around the horn of her sidesaddle.

"I rode south looking for the Mexican," Buck said. "He made me look like a fool. I was ready to defend him—free—and he broke jail. A man has honor, you know."

She laughed shortly. "I disagree. To me, a *lawyer* is not a *man*. He is a fraud and shyster, nothing more."

Buck doffed his hat. "I thank you, Mrs. Twiggs. Your tongue needs no hypodermic, like the veins of your poor husband. Nor does it need to be sharpened, madam."

"What do you want, McKee?"

"Why was Wadsworth Matthews murdered?"

"Murdered?" Her brows rose. "The coroner's inquest decided he'd committed suicide, remember?"

"A framed verdict, Mrs. Twiggs."

Her voice dripped honey. "Why is the late Mr. Matthews so important to you, Lawyer McKee? He was a possible client, nothing more, was he not?"

Buck said pointedly, "There's money here somewhere. Somebody is making lots of money."

Her frown showed puzzlement, then her gay laugh echoed. "There are times, Mr. McKee, when I doubt your sanity, because you shift the topic of conversation very rapidly many times. Your mind is apparently unable to stay on one single subject."

She played with him skillfully. Buck held his stirrings of anger, although he wanted to shake her.

What had taken place since he had last seen her, twisting her silk handkerchief, in the Yellowstone City livery barn, with a look of lost bewilderment on her lovely face?

She had been soft and womanly then; now she was cold and hard. She was as emotionless as Marcia Andrews, as entirely without mercy. Buck realized that further conversation would only be wasted.

"I bid you farewell, Mrs. Twiggs," he said.

"You are leaving, Mr. McKee? Leaving for good?"

"For good, Mrs. Twiggs."

For one moment, her eyes lost their hardness and became the eyes of a lost girl again, and Buck felt the spearings of hope. But this was short-lived, because the veil came down immediately over her blue eyes.

"I wish you well, Mr. McKee."

"I wish you and Mr. Twiggs the same, Mrs. Twiggs. You should make Miss Andrews stop injecting opium or one of its derivatives into the veins of your husband, though."

She stared, eyes bulging. "Then you knew, Mr. McKee?"

"A blind man could see that." Buck tried a shot in the dark. "Wadsworth Matthews's arms, too, were needle-marked. He also had the dope habit. Perhaps it led to his murder?"

"Mr. McKee—"

"Mrs. Twiggs . . ." Buck said gently.

She broke up then. Sobs tore from her throat. She gasped, "I'm a lone woman—all alone. I can't do what a man can do. No woman can. . . ."

Buck reined close, and rested her blonde head on his chest, his arms gently around her. Finally she raised her head, daubing her eyes with a small handkerchief.

"There is one thing I cannot understand, Mr. McKee. I seem to sense a former relationship—friendship, if I may say it—between dead Mr. Matthews and the Mexican and you."

Buck stiffened. Had her weeping been a mere act? He had told a few women too much before in his life, and paid the penalty.

"You read something into this that is not there," he said.

"I'm a coward, Mr. McKee. I've feared death, and I've allowed dope and an evil woman to bring my husband close to death. I've told you I love my husband dearly. I told you no lie. But does it look like love when the one who loves is afraid to sacrifice for her loved one?"

"Who would kill you, Mrs. Twiggs?"

"I don't know. Any man on Circle Five could be suspected. I've never been threatened, Mr. McKee. But it's there—in the very air—"

"Invariably, money sires evil," Buck McKee said, "and where is the money behind this evil?"

"I don't know. Maybe some of the Circle Five hands are rustling Circle Five steers?"

"That could be so."

"I've suspected a few Circle Five riders. I'll not name names because I have no outright evidence. But I am no cowboy, nor can I follow a trail, Mr. McKee."

"You've tried, I take it?"

"First, I tried trailing days. Cowboys came back and asked me where I was going and could they help me. Then I tried nights. I couldn't trail a shooting star across a midnight sky!"

"Have you called upon Sheriff Jenkins?"

"Sheriff Jenkins, at heart, is a good man, but he's lost his contacts with the outside world. He's blind. He can't feel, smell, taste, or hear."

"Maybe the other side has bought him off?"

"Only intelligent people sell out, Mr. McKee. The ignorant cling to false idols. If I had some proof, I'd go to Sheriff Jenkins."

"And what would he do?"

"He'd help me, I feel sure. He'd serve any warrant

I issued. He'd do it not out of loyalty to me. He'd do it because it was his job. If that Mexican hangs around this range, Sheriff Jenkins will get him in time."

Buck was acquiring a new estimation of Sheriff Jenkins. He decided he had heard enough. He wouldn't tip his hand to this woman. She was still an unknown factor.

"I am talking about something that concerns me not a bit," he told Louise Twiggs. "I am leaving for good, lady. My sympathy is yours."

"Could I hire you—pay you—"

Louise Twiggs never completed her sentence. Hard hoofs drummed toward her and Buck. Buck roweled his bronc into the thick timber. He dismounted and came back on foot, hand on his gun.

Rocky Pincus and Blacky Jordan drew rein in a cloud of dust, their horses sliding to a halt.

"We came in early from work," the Circle Five range boss said, "and we heard you'd headed for town alone. It isn't safe for a woman to ride abroad alone, Mrs. Twiggs. That crazy Mexican is still loose, you know."

Had Rocky Pincus been alone, Buck would have jumped him—and the same held true for Blacky Jordan—but Buck McKee was too wise not to know the odds were against him.

Louise Twiggs smiled sweetly. "How nice of you boys."

The trio rode toward Yellowstone City.

Chapter Fifteen

Two nights later, Tortilla Joe darted into an alley and flattened himself against a dark concrete wall. He was in the military post of Fort Assiniboine.

He had seen a stocky man suddenly turn the corner. The kerosene street lamps, smoking on high poles, had reflected off a bit of shiny metal on the man's vest. And Tortilla Joe knew a law badge when he saw one.

He had also recognized Sheriff Jenkins immediately. The Mexican scowled. What was the Yellowstone City sheriff doing in this military post, over fifty miles east of Yellowstone City? Fort Assiniboine was not in Sheriff Jenkins's county.

Tortilla Joe's blood suddenly froze. Had the Yellowstone City sheriff trailed him to Fort Assiniboine? Tortilla Joe suddenly wished he were north of the Canadian line. Up in Alberta province.

Common sense returned. He was an escaped murderer. Escaped murderers, with the least bit of brains, didn't ride into populated areas, especially one like Fort Assiniboine where anybody who didn't wear a cavalry uniform wore an Assiniboine Indian blanket.

A civilian in Fort Assiniboine stood out like a bandaged thumb.

What was Sheriff Jenkins doing in Fort Assini-

boine? He had not ridden here for a telegraph wire.
Blacky Jordan had especially ridden to Malta to get
to the telegraph, to spread the word that a murderer
had broken out of jail in Yellowstone City.

Tortilla Joe decided to play it smart. He pulled
out of town to his rimrock camp to the south.

He had reached this area last night, pushing the
entire distance from Yellowstone City in just a day
and a few hours. Today, he had been questioning
local ranchers at their home ranches.

Yes, Fort Assiniboine bought beef. That was nat-
ural, wasn't it? Soldiers needed meat. Redskins had
to have their beef rations. Where was this beef
brought?

A few head had been sold to Uncle Sam by the
local ranchers, but most of the beef apparently was
driven in from outside ranches. No rancher had
made inquiries as to who sold the most beef to the
government.

"Talk with Ike Sutton," one rancher said. "He's
the army sutler who buys all Fort Assiniboine's beef."

Tortilla Joe nodded, but he didn't look up Ike
Sutton, although he had the big beefy man pointed
out to him on Fort Assiniboine's main street.

"That Sutton sure can kick out a buckin' bronc,"
a townsman said. "Ol'-time cowboy from Arizona
Territory, they tell me. He knows beef, too."

Tortilla Joe scouted Fort Assiniboine. The slaughterhouse was along Milk River in the trees, the offal
being thrown into the river.

Tortilla Joe, though, wasn't interested in a cow's
intestines; his interest lay in the hide that had en-

cased those intestines—especially in the brand that
the hide sported, for the majority of these cowhides
might bear the Circle Five iron.

Next morning at eight, squatted among the boulders, field glasses on the trail below, he saw Sheriff Jenkins push toward Yellowstone City. The sheriff had
spent the night in Fort Assiniboine.

Why?

Tortilla Joe went back to his grazing horse, saddled and bridled him, and rode off the rimrock. With
his horse sliding in shale, the Mexican braced himself solidly in Visalia stirrups, his stocky front pushing hard against the wide fork of the Garcia saddle.

He skirted the south edge of the military post, listening to the rat-a-tat of a parade bugle, and rode
along the river, keeping hidden by the high brush.
His nose soon told him the slaughterhouse was directly ahead.

He dismounted, tied his horse to a sapling, and
went ahead on foot after taking off his Sacramento
silver-mounted spurs, hanging them over his saddle
horn.

He didn't know what to expect. From his high perch
on the rimrock he had looked down on the slaughterhouse's holding pens, but only a few scrub calves had
been there. Evidently, the slaughterhouse had no beef
on hand to kill at present.

Downriver about two miles was an encampment of
Assiniboine and Sioux—and maybe a few Gros Ven-
tres—evidently awaiting supplies from the Indian
agency.

The presence of the redskins told Tortilla Joe that a

beef kill had just been made or was soon to be made. He favored the latter assumption.

Logic told him that if a beef ration had already been issued, the redskins would have jerked their beef and moved back on their home grounds, their bellies full and larders overrunning.

No, the beef kill was yet to come.

He followed a trail that wound along the river's south bank. Boots and moccasins had made the path, along with the pads of cottontails. He rounded a bend and came upon two squaws sitting on the bank, fishing.

He stopped, intending to retreat, but it was too late, for the squaws had seen him. He decided to blunder through in some way. He knew little if anything about these Northern Plains Indians.

He held up his right hand, palm out. "How," he said.

One squaw was middle-aged and very fat, wearing voluminous clothes, but the other was young, with black hair hanging in braids, her lithe body clothed in finely tailored buckskin, and she was the one who laughed.

"What's so funny?" Tortilla Joe asked, slightly irritated.

"We speak English," the fat squaw said. "We both go to the Reservation School."

"You're too old to go to school," Tortilla Joe told her.

"Never too old to learn," the squaw said, peering at him. "You an Indian?"

"Why say that?" Tortilla asked.

"Your skin is dark."

Evidently, the two had never seen a Mexican. Tortilla Joe decided that was a point in his favor. Now no squaw would report having seen a Mexican hanging around.

"I'm Apache," Tortilla Joe said. "From down in Arizona Territory."

Apparently, neither knew where the Arizona Territory was, nor had they heard of the Apache tribe.

"You here for the beef ration?" the young squaw asked.

Tortilla Joe liked her. She had a wide, happy-looking face, and he wondered, idly, if she knew how to pound out a *tortilla*. He had not had a tortilla, except for the one he made himself, since he had left Juarez months ago.

Then he realized she wouldn't know how to palm out a *tortilla*. These Indians, he had heard, ate corn pone, or bread made of wheat.

"I'd like a little beef," he said. "When are the steers coming in?"

"Three or four more days," the older squaw said. "I hope we get fat beef this time. Last beef was old and stringy."

"Where does the beef come from?"

Neither of the squaws knew. They were given the hides, and both said the brands were always cut out of the hides. And if you didn't know what brand a beef had carried, you didn't know where he came from, did you?

"Why are the brands cut out?" the Mexican asked, playing ignorant, and both squaws laughed.

"Why do you think?" the young one asked, dark eyes dancing. Did they hold a challenge?

"I haven't the slightest idea," Tortilla Joe said, still pretending ignorance.

"Maybe the sutler bought the beef from somebody who stole it?" the old squaw said, and both laughed again.

"I never heard of such a thing," Tortilla Joe said.

Again the laughter, and then, from the young squaw, "All army sutlers are thieves that steal from both the Indians and Uncle Sam. They buy the poorest beef at the lowest prices. Then they charge Washington for the best beef at highest prices."

Tortilla Joe nodded, listening carefully.

"The Indian goes with an empty belly. Uncle Sam pays for beef he never gets. The sutler gets rich quick. All sutlers are thieves," the young one repeated.

"Not all," the older squaw said.

"Show me one who isn't?" the younger girl challenged.

"Get me a shovel and we'll dig up one somewhere."

Again laughter. Tortilla Joe said, "The only honest one is a dead one, huh? What do they do with the brands?"

Both squaws shrugged. Just then, by coincidence, both lines had bites. Dark hands began pulling in fishlines. Tortilla Joe took advantage of the moment to beat his unnoticed escape.

He had learned a lot. Evidently, sutler Ike Sutton was of the same mold as that of his sutler contemporaries, another thief getting rich fast.

Squatting in the brush, Tortilla Joe studied the slaughterhouse, his eyes thoughtful.

The long log building with a sod roof ran directly along the riverbank, its platforms hanging over the river. From these platforms offal and hoofs and other inedibles were dumped directly into the water. Were the sections of hides bearing brands also thrown into the swirling, muddy Milk River?

Tortilla Joe doubted this. If the brands were thrown into the river, some might be washed up on sandbars and the bank, and found and identified.

No, the brand sections were either given an acid bath or buried. Burning them in a fire would do little good, for green cowhide is almost impossible to burn.

Tortilla Joe decided to go swimming. Within a few minutes, naked as the day he was born, the Mexican was in Milk River's warm water, drifting downstream toward the pilings of the slaughterhouse's platforms.

A short unshaven man came out on one platform, glaring down at the Mexican, who had caught the piling. Tortilla Joe looked up at the man. "The current is fast," he said.

"What're you doin' in the river, Injun?"

Tortilla Joe deliberately made his English poor. "Onct the river she was mine," he pointed out.

"Yeah, once," the man said sarcastically, "but not any longer, redskin. Uncle Sam owns the river now. Don't hang around this slaughterhouse, savvy?"

"For why not?"

"Not just healthy, savvy?"

"You are too small to make me go away."

"Okay, Injun, okay. Maybe I'm tougher than you think, huh? Sure, I'm here alone now, but one toot of the whistle, and help will come from the post."

Tortilla Joe had found out what he wanted to: this man was alone. "I want no troubles," he said, and swam upstream, rounded the bend, climbed onto the grassy bank, and dressed, grinning to himself. Within a few minutes, he had circled the slaughterhouse and was inside it.

Through a dirty window he looked at the calves in the corral. They were skinny, underfed, bony little bovines, and none carried a brand, so the Mexican learned nothing from them.

The place smelled putrid, and the stench cut his nostrils. Dried blood stained the dirt floor, turning the sod bone hard. Tracks of boots and shoes showed through the bloodstains.

Pulleys hung from the track overhead. No skinned carcasses were in evidence, but this was only logical. Meat wouldn't keep overnight in this late summer heat. Cattle had to be killed and dressed out immediately at this time of the year, or their meat would spoil. This meant that minutes after the kill, beef would be in the hands of the squaws who would strip it and hang it and dry it. Some would be ground into chokecherries and suet for *pemmican*.

Within ten minutes, Tortilla Joe had gone through the entire slaughterhouse—and found no hides. He searched for a vat or pit where brands would be thrown into acid, but he knew the slaughterhouse held no such pit. For if it had, he knew the stench of acid would be strong. Brands were evidently freighted away and buried somewhere.

But where?

He grinned mirthlessly. Around him stretched thousands of acres of wilderness. Unless a man caught the stench, he would never be able to find the burial spot of the brands.

And he knew that sutler Ike Sutton would bury the brands very, very deep to make them safe from the clawing paws of coyotes and town dogs.

He heard the sound of boots. That would be the arrogant little man who had challenged him. Gun raised, grinning, the Mexican drew back behind a door casing as he heard the boots coming in his direction.

"Dang it," the man said, "I'm sure I heard a noise in here."

Tortilla Joe heard the man move something in the next room. "Can't be mice I heard," the man said, "because a mouse can't make that much noise."

Tortilla Joe suddenly holstered his gun, the image of the arrogant blowhard man limned in his memory. Much as he desired to buffalo the man cold, logic told him not to.

Far better that the man never know that anybody had invaded the slaughterhouse while he had been on guard. It was best to have no suspicions raised.

Carefully Tortilla Joe tiptoed through another door and found himself in the timber. He darted into the brush, hunkered, watched a slaughterhouse window, and saw the man move past it without looking outside. The man hadn't seen him.

Tortilla Joe went to his horse. Within a few minutes, he was riding back toward Yellowstone City, a sour taste in his mouth.

He had learned nothing here. His long ride had been for naught, except that he had seen Sheriff Jenkins.

He had darned little to tell Buck McKee.

Chapter Sixteen

BUCK had not seen Sheriff Jenkins leave Yellowstone City, as the lawman had left at night, but Buck did see the sheriff ride in from Fort Assiniboine.

Fear touched the Texan. Had Sheriff Jenkins been out scouting, and had the lawman cut Tortilla Joe's trail? And followed Tortilla Joe into Fort Assiniboine?

No, Jenkins rode alone. Had Jenkins arrested the Mexican, Tortilla Joe would have trailed the sheriff, a lead rope running from the Mexican's horse to the sheriff's saddle horn, and Tortilla Joe's hands tied behind his back, his boots lashed to the stirrups.

Had the sheriff killed Tortilla Joe? Buck doubted that. If Tortilla Joe had been gunned down, his body would have been over his saddle, hands and feet tied to the stirrups, while Sheriff Jenkins led the Mexican's horse.

Buck then remembered that Fort Assiniboine was

in a different county than Yellowstone City. If Tortilla Joe was killed in Fort Assiniboine, his body would undoubtedly be held in the military post for a coroner's inquest.

Buck McKee suddenly grinned.

He had never seen Sheriff Jenkins draw, but he had seen the sheriff buckle on his gun belt—a slow process for Jenkins's big hands.

Sheriff Jenkins was very slow of foot and movement. Buck knew full well the deadly gun-prowess of his Mexican companion.

Tortilla Joe was one of the fastest men with rifle or pistol. Buck figured that the slow-moving, slow-witted Sheriff Jenkins wouldn't have a chance if he matched Tortilla Joe gun to gun.

Buck still crouched on the rimrock overlooking Circle Five, but he could see Yellowstone City clearly in his glasses, for the high altitude air was crystal clear.

Sheriff Jenkins rode into town and stabled his bronc in the county barn behind the courthouse, then bowlegged into his office. Deputy Sheriff Isaac Watson met his boss at the door.

Buck wondered what cock-and-bull story Watson had told his superior to explain the condition of his face, for Buck new that his fists had wreaked damage on the arrogant deputy's face. Probably told Jenkins his horse had bucked him off, Buck thought, and grinned.

He had seen a strange thing happen at dawn this morning on Circle Five. Ramrod Rocky Pincus and Blacky Jordan had ridden into the ranch at the crack of dawn.

The two didn't ride openly into the big spread. They rode in hidden by timber and came in behind the barn. Then they had sneaked to the bunkhouse, using the blacksmith shop and other buildings to shield them from the house.

One hour later, Rocky had been in the yard, giving orders to his crew. Blacky Jordan was not in sight. After sending his crew about their chores, Rocky had returned to his bunkhouse, and Buck had not seen him since.

Evidently, Rocky and Blacky were sleeping. Buck could come to no other conclusion. And if they were sleeping, that meant they had pounded leather all night. Doing what?

Hard-working, honest cowboys rode days and slept nights. Rocky Pincus and Blacky Jordan apparently had reversed the process, which meant, maybe, that they weren't honest cowboys.

Raw impatience rasped Buck McKee. He thought of Canada. He wanted to be riding toward Canuck territory. He and Tortilla Joe had picked Wad Matthews's farm to meet at, and to visit a few hours with Wad, nothing more.

His grub supply was running low. He itched from lack of a bath. He needed a shave. Whiskers curled in and tormented his jaw. Unless this thing was brought to a head soon, he would have to break into another Circle Five line camp for supplies.

He dozed, eyes on the ranch below. Riders came and went, and again Louise Twiggs watered her plants, dipping up buckets of water from the windmill's tank, the windmill fan gently turning in the eternal Montana wind.

Buck had never been in a country that had this much wind. One day the wind blew for North Dakota, and the next day it returned to Idaho, where it turned right around and headed back for North Dakota again to repeat the process.

The only calm moments were at sunrise and at sunset. Then, millions of mosquitoes rose from the river and creeks and water holes, driving range horses mad. Range horses ran and ran until the wind rose again and drove the mosquitoes away.

Louise Twiggs always wore mosquito netting hanging from her wide straw hat. The backs of Buck's hands had been chewed into lumps, and his face was not much better off.

A terriffic heat hung to the rangelands. One night there was a thunderstorm. Lightning flared, thunder roared—and not a drop of rain fell, although black clouds swarmed overhead.

The rain had fallen miles away, though, for Buck soon smelled the good perfume of damp earth wafted in the wind.

Marcia Andrews rode to the ranch at five-thirty that afternoon, Buck's glasses showing her redheaded loveliness clearly. She rode astraddle her saddle this time, the way a cowboy rode.

Buck admired her seat in her saddle. Her black bag was tied behind her cantle. Louise Twiggs was in the yard when Marcia rode in. Marcia entered the house alone, Mrs. Twiggs remaining with her roses. Soon the redhead came out and mounted, two Circle Five cowboys riding back to Yellowstone City with her.

Buck had asked Mrs. Twiggs why she hadn't stopped Marcia from giving Old Man Twiggs the injections. She said she had ordered the redhead to stop, but Marcia had paid no attention.

The next time Marcia had tried to inject dope into Old Man Twiggs, Louise had lunged forward, but two Circle Five cowboys had held her back.

Buck had asked her the name of the two men. Smoky Smith and Jack Olson, the blonde had said. Smith and Olson were firm friends of Rocky Pincus, as was another Circle Five rider, Martin Breckinridge. All of them had been in the Broken Cinch the day Buck had the fight there.

Heat grew with the rising sun; the sun heeled over, and still the heat hung. Lightning played occasionally to the west. The very air was heavy and dense.

Sweat pasted Buck's shirt to his back. His canteen was getting empty. His horse needed water, too. Dusk finally came. Toward midnight, there would be a moon. Darkness settled in. Darkness found Buck McKee squatting beside Circle Five's barn, his horse hidden in the brush.

A slow wind sighed in the eaves of the barn. The collies were locked in the ranch house yard. Occasionally one barked in response to a coyote.

Buck heard horses chewing hay through the wall behind him. His thigh muscles ached from squatting. He wished he knew who had murdered Wad Matthews. Then he could accost the man, either take him in to Sheriff Jenkins or force the man to draw, and have it over with—and then he and Tortilla Joe could ride on.

But there was more to be done than that. Tortilla Joe must be cleared of the murder charge dangling over him.

Suddenly Buck stiffened, aching muscles forgotten. Boots approached. Cautious boots, quiet boots. Then he saw the dim outlines of two men approaching.

He recognized big Rocky Pincus immediately. The other outline was more lithe, younger. That had to be Blacky Jordan. The two men entered the barn, passing no more than fifteen feet away. Buck held his breath.

He started breathing when he heard horses move in the barn, as though being led from the stalls. He waited to hear the slap of leather as saddles were slung up, but no slap came. He heard saddle leather creak; somebody mounted a bronc inside the barn.

Silently Buck glided through the night, reached the willows, found his horse and slung up, his gun harness creaking slightly. Which direction would Pincus and Jordan take?

They had ridden in from the northeast. Would they ride out in that same direction?

Buck quickly circled sleeping Circle Five, finally stationing his horse east of the ranch in the brush. He dismounted and held his hand over his bronc's nose.

Long rolling thunder sounded in the south. Chain lightning played against massive black clouds. Again Buck McKee waited . . . but this time, not for long. . . .

Two riders swept past, horses running hard, heading for the high northeastern lifts of mighty Circle Five's enormous range. They thundered past, out of hearing distance of the ranch house, and then the dark Montana night swallowed them.

Their hoofbeats echoed, then died; by now, Buck McKee was in the saddle, and he frowned, sitting on a horse that pulled against his bit, as he wanted to chase the two horses that had just loped past.

Buck's frown deepened. There was no use trying to trail Rocky Pincus and Blacky Jordan. The ink-black night made this impossible. And by the time the laggard moon arose, the Circle Five pair would be many, many miles away, mere dots moving under yellow light across an immense continent.

Then once again Buck McKee stiffened, listening. From the direction of Circle Five came other approaching hoofbeats as other riders pushed northeast into the dark night.

The riders swept by. Hard-riding men, deep in saddles, their horses breathing hard. The rattle of hoofs, the harsh sounds of leather creaking, the riders, were gone, trailing Pincus and Jordan into inky blackness.

Buck remembered Louise Twiggs saying that Rocky Pincus had three close friends among Circle Five cowboys—Smoky Smith, Jack Olson, and Martin Breckinridge.

Were these the riders who had just passed? Were they also involved in this dangerous web of conspiracy? They had come from the direction of Circle Five. That meant they were also on the Twiggs's payroll.

Buck listened, but heard no more approaching riders. When the moon heeled over the hills, golden and bright, he was far to the northeast, but the trail was cold—he discovered nothing, as he told Tortilla Joe when the Mexican returned from Fort Assiniboine.

"They cut the brands from the hides," the Mexican said, "and then they sell the hides to the redskins to make moccasins and clothes out of."

"Circle Five burns on the right shoulder," Buck said.

"The squaws told me the right shoulder of each hide is missing. That means they've cut out the Circle Five iron. I don't know where they put the parts they cut out, though. I couldn't find an acid pit."

"Prob'ly bury them somewhere in the night," Buck said. "What was Sheriff Jenkins doing in Fort Assiniboine?"

"I don't know, Buckshot. I hid fast and in a hurry, believe you me. I am getting tired of running and not acting like a man, *amigo*."

"You got company," Buck said. "You think maybe Sheriff Jenkins is suspicious that Circle Five loses cattle?"

"If he is, it has taken him a long time to get moving. The squaws told me that the right shoulder of the hides has been cut out for quite a few beef issues."

"Maybe Louise Twiggs talked to him," Buck said, and told Tortilla Joe about the five riders that had left Circle Five in the dark of the night.

"I bet you a Sonora adobe *peso* that they rode out to gather Circle Five beef. Those Indians at the Fort expect a beef ration any day now."

Buck nodded.

Tortilla Joe's voice was heavy. "And I'll bet another adobe *peso* that a few days ago not five but six rode, and the sixth was our old friend, Wadsworth Matthews!"

Chapter Seventeen

SHERIFF Jenkins was in a sour mood. Things had been going bad lately. What had been an easy-chair job had become a saddle job. It had all started with Circle Five burning down this damned farmer. Then that lawyer had to come into town.

Time was when all he had to do was go to his office, pick up his fishing pole, go down to the river and doze on the grassy bank while he fished for catfish. But those days, it seemed, were gone forever; there was the Mexican to catch, and now Louise Twiggs had come up with the idea that Circle Five was losing cattle.

Sheriff Jenkins was a man who never cared to disturb the status quo. If things ran calmly and smoothly, he felt it was best to let them remain as they were.

Now, seated in his hot office, the sheriff thought of his long ride to Fort Assiniboine and of his talk with the sheriff there about cattle possibly going from Circle Five graze to the public slaughterhouse in Fort Peck.

The Fort Assiniboine sheriff had assured his fellow peace officer that he would post a deputy to dog the sutler, Ike Sutton, for he was the only man in Fort Assiniboine who bought cattle.

Sheriff Jenkins had been too wise to ask the slaughterhouse boss when the next kill would be brought about, but he knew that the kill-yards would soon butcher. When Indians came into reservation headquarters, they came because of one of two things: either to raise trouble or to get beef rations.

The Fort Assiniboine redskins had been peaceful, so Sheriff Jenkins judged a beef kill was soon in order.

Deputy Sheriff Isaac Watson looked in, saw all was well, nodded and left, boots clomping into the distance. Sheriff Jenkins gave a brief thought to his one and only deputy.

Watson was a distant relative of Old Man Twiggs. Before the owner of Circle Five had become sick, he had asked Sheriff Jenkins to give Isaac Watson a job, and the sheriff had instantly complied.

Sheriff Jenkins had known that Isaac Watson had been of no account when he had sworn in the deputy, but Sheriff Jenkins was, above all, a minor politician. Old Man Twiggs could have asked him for the moon, and he would have done his best to deliver.

The motivation was simple. Old Man Twiggs was the county's biggest taxpayer. He paid more taxes than the rest of the county's citizens combined.

Old Man Twiggs, then, paid Sheriff Jenkins's salary, and Old Man Twiggs's distant relative could have a job any time he wanted it. Wasn't Old Man Twiggs's

Circle Five, in reality, paying Deputy Sheriff Isaac Watson's salary?

Sheriff Jenkins wondered where Watson had got the beaten-up face. Watson had a black eye, his lips were swollen, and his jaw showed black and blue spots.

Watson claimed his horse had bucked him off. "Danged critter just busted in two, and him an old well-broke saddler. Buck me off headfirst—no, face first!—into a pile of boulders, Sheriff!"

Sheriff Jenkins didn't believe that. He had seen men who had been thrown from broncs to land on their faces. He had also seen men beaten up in fist fights, and Watson's face looked as if fists—not stones —had hammered it.

But the lawman spent little time thinking of Deputy Sheriff Watson, for Watson was expendable—he didn't count; but what did count was the continued vote of Circle Five, since this vote kept him, Sheriff Jenkins, on this easy job.

Were rustlers really hitting Circle Five? Or had Louise Twiggs, like all women, just gone off on a crazy streak?

He realized he had not paid enough attention lately to Old Man Twiggs. He glanced up as lovely redheaded Marcia Andrews, sitting sidesaddle on a magnificent blue roan, rode past his office, her small black doctor's bag tied behind the saddle.

Marcia lifted a small gloved hand and showed him a nice smile, but the sheriff noticed that her eyes, even from this distance, were as cold and scornful as always.

He grunted, and lifted his hat. The girl rode on and went out of view, and Sheriff Jenkins again thought of Old Man Twiggs.

What ailed the old cowman, anyway? And why did he let this girl treat him? Marcia Andrews was a pharmacist, not a doctor of medicine.

Occasionally a doctor came over from Malta, or an army doctor happened in from Fort Assiniboine. Next time a genuine doctor came to Yellowstone City, he would get the doctor to look at Old Man Twiggs—and learn the truth.

Sheriff Jenkins got to his feet. Much as he hated to move on such a hot day, he had to act as if he were still looking for the Mexican, who he hoped had made his escape into Canada by now.

Within a short time, he drew rein and looked at the ruins of Wadsworth Matthews's farm, paying especial attention to the corral. Apparently, some idiot—or idiots—had spaded up the area inside the pole fence, and had, indeed, taken down the fence, too—even to digging up the posts.

Sheriff Jenkins dismounted, shaking his head slowly. What loco had done this, and why? He dropped his reins, ground-tying his horse, and walked out, kicking first at this clod, then that pile of dirt, wondering just why anybody would go to such great labor, and for what apparent purpose.

He stopped beside a hole made by one of the corral's gateposts, which now lay on its side. He had figured that some farmer had taken down the fence because of its posts, and because fence posts could be made out of the rails, but all rails and posts lay as they had fallen.

The farmer might have gone home for a team and wagon to haul the rails and posts, but Sheriff Jenkins couldn't see why the corral's interior had been spaded.

Idly, he kicked a clod; it rolled to one side. He turned to leave, then hesitated, for something golden shiny on the ground caught his eye. Bending to pick up this object, he suddenly realized he held a new shiny twenty-dollar gold piece.

What the—?

He turned the gold piece between thumb and forefinger. It looked as new as if it had just come from the mint. He looked at the date. The date was the present year. Somebody had lost a gold piece?

He frowned. The gold piece had been *under* the dirt, not on top of it. If the gold piece had dropped from a pocket, it wouldn't be buried. It would have lain on *top* of the clod!

Sheriff Jenkins hurriedly dropped to his knees, his arm going into the post hole. He felt around inside carefully. He found no more gold pieces, but he did find a hollowed area to the side of the hole—a cavity in the earth.

He suddenly remembered an article he had recently read. There had been no banks in early Texas, of course. When a cowman sold a bunch of cattle, he naturally had a supply of gold, which he had to hide from bandits.

The usual hiding place was in a corral. Naturally, a man made some signs when he dug a hole and buried something. But in a corral, horses or cattle running around inside soon pounded the earth flat, killing all tracks and signs of digging.

Therefore, the early cowmen usually hid their gold in their corrals, but buried it close to one particular post so they would be able to relocate it easily; for if the gold were buried in the corral's interior, a man might forget and have to dig and dig . . . and then maybe never find his treasure.

He also remembered hearing that Wadsworth Matthews had been reared in Texas, or had lived there at one time.

Wadsworth Matthews had had a cache of gold in a hole beside this uprooted corral gatepost. Somebody had dug it out, not knowing that his shovel had also thrown out the gold piece now resting in Sheriff Jenkins's pants pocket.

Now where would a poor dirt farmer like Wadsworth Matthews get a cache of gold coins? Had a bank been held up lately around this area?

Reports from other sheriffs' offices had reported no bank holdups in Montana for many years. How about train holdups, then? No, there had been no train robberies for a long, long time, either.

Sheriff Jenkins's eyes went still narrower. Thieves fell out at times, didn't they? And Rocky Pincus, for no apparent reason, had led Circle Five against the Matthews farm—and hadn't Matthews been killed while sick in bed in the hotel?

Sheriff Jenkins had no real faith in the conclusion that Matthews had shot himself. He was of the opinion, privately, that somebody had murdered Matthews, but as long as the coroner's jury had returned a verdict of suicide, it was all right with him. Because of that verdict, his office didn't have to search for a killer.

Had Matthews been connected with the cattle thieves that Louise Twiggs suspected of working on Circle Five range? And had this new shiny twenty-dollar gold piece served as payment to Matthews for stolen cattle?

And who had spaded and pulled posts and gone off with the cache that Matthews had had in his post hole?

Sheriff Jenkins mounted his horse, looked back at the spaded area, and rode off. He then questioned every farmer, asking if he had pulled down the corral, but each one said he had had nothing to do with it. But finally one did say, "I know who did it, though, Sheriff."

"Who?"

"A woman an' a man. I was huntin' my ol' milk cow. Had my field glasses along. Saw them workin' there, but I was a mile or so away."

"Did you recognize either or both of them, Sig?"

"Look, Sheriff, a mile is a long ways—and my glasses ain't very powerful—"

"I asked you a question, Sig. I expect an answer."

"I wouldn't swear this in court, understand, but the man—I didn't know him, but I did recognize the woman."

"Who was she?"

"She looked to me like she was Wad Matthews's wife, Sheriff."

"Thanks, Sig."

Sheriff Jenkins continued riding toward Yellowstone City. Dusk was sneaking in, and the heat was diminishing slowly. He swatted mosquitoes from his bronc's sweaty shoulder.

He had always liked Mrs. Matthews. Friendly little woman, always with a cheery *Hello, Sheriff Jenkins,* and not surly and suspicious like some of the farmers' wives.

He had seen Mrs. Matthews when he had been in Malta, and had met her new husband. He seemed like a nice guy, the new man, and he had wished them both well.

Evidently, Mrs. Matthews—the ex-Mrs. Matthews, he corrected himself—had suspected her husband of having this gold cache, but hadn't known just where in the corral it had been.

Therefore, she and her husband had first spaded the corral, then pulled down the posts and thus found the gold cache.

Sheriff Jenkins wondered if the woman would know anything about her husband's connections with any nefarious work that would pay him in gold to this quantity.

Maybe he had best ride to Malta to talk with the ex-Mrs. Matthews.

He pulled his horse in on a hill. The wind was rising again, driving away the pesky mosquitoes. He summed things up. Matthews hadn't brought this gold with him from South Dakota. Jenkins felt sure of that.

The gold hadn't come from a bank or train robbery. It had to come from rustling cattle. Maybe Louise Twiggs was right?

He considered the situation. Malta was miles and miles to the northwest. His horse, though, was fresh. He would reach the cow town by sunrise. And he needed to get out of Yellowstone City for a day or so, too. A man could stand the same area for just so long.

He reined his bronc toward Malta.

Chapter Eighteen

BUCK McKEE squatted in the high boulders and watched Sheriff Jenkins head northwest across the country, his bronc at a long trot. Buck lowered his field glasses and frowned.

The sheriff could only be riding to Malta. There were no ranches or farmers in the direction the lawman rode. There was only open range between here and Malta.

Why did Jenkins ride toward the cow town?

He and Tortilla Joe talked it over later on when they met on the rimrock overlooking Cache Creek. "He's going to check at the railroad depot," Tortilla Joe said, "to see if there are any answers to the telegram he had Blacky Jordan send out—the wire asking other lawmen to be on the lookout for me."

Buck shook his head. "I can't agree, Tortilla. If a

wire came in, the Malta sheriff would send somebody to Yellowstone City with it."

Tortilla Joe's heavy shoulders shrugged. "Well, he rides in that direction, Buckshot. By sunrise he should be in Malta. You want me to trail him?"

Buck grinned sourly. "There won't be a moon until around midnight, and a man can't scout range at night without a moon, so good luck, *amigo*, but don't follow him all the way into town, savvy?"

"Why not?"

"You might get picked up by the law in Malta, you fool."

"Thanks for the compliment." Tortilla Joe mounted and rode toward Malta, leaving Buck alone on the rimrock.

Buck McKee scratched his whiskers thoughtfully. How many days had he and Tortilla Joe scouted this northeast section of Circle Five? When would he and his partner be free to head north into Canada?

At first, they had seen scattered bands of Circle Five cattle—steers, cows, calves. During the night, riders had cut back the cows and calves. Soon the small herds consisted only of steers. Gradually the small herds were being worked into one big herd.

Five Circle Five riders worked the cattle. Rocky Pincus. Blacky Jordan. Smoky Smith. Jack Olson. Martin Breckinridge. They worked nights, slept days.

When would the stolen herd be moved and sold? The cattle, Buck realized, would go to the butcher knives at Fort Assiniboine, for the herd was being built in the northeast, almost on the reservation limits of Fort Assiniboine.

The herd would have to be jumped when delivered to crooked sutler Ike Sutton, or there would be no evidence of thievery. What if the five were jumped while working Circle Five cattle?

There would be no evidence that they intended to steal these steers. All five men drew Twiggs's wages. And a cowboy's job is to move cattle, to push stock on to better water and higher grass, to ride bog holes, to pull out bogged-down cattle.

Once the steers were off Circle Five grass and being driven in a herd, then there would be evidence that they were being stolen.

Buck wasn't interested in stopping the Circle Five rustling. He was now sure that Wad Matthews had helped in this rustling. He was equally sure somebody—maybe one of the five rustlers?—had put a bullet into Wad's brain to silence him.

And a murder charge hung over Tortilla Joe's dark-haired head. "Before I ride on," the Mexican had said, "I will find out who killed Whitey Jordan, for sure. I didn't do it, Buck."

Buck had pointed out that Tortilla Joe had said he had seen Wadsworth Matthews point his rifle at Whitey Jordan's heart.

"I have thought that over, Buckshot. I remember looking at Whitey layin' there dead. And the hole in his heart was a big one. Now that I think of it, a rifle would have made just a little blue hole—especially Wad's rifle, for he was shooting steel-jacketed bullets."

"We're in danger, pal," Buck had said. "Jenkins

may look dumb, but I don't think he's as stupid as he looks."

"Or pretends," Tortilla Joe added.

Now Buck drifted back toward Circle Five, lying far to the southwest. He could do nothing here in this heavy darkness. Chain lightning played far to the south, he noticed, along the Missouri river. Rain was falling over there.

Buck knew that the lightning made things stand out clearly for a few brief seconds, and he wished a rainstorm would hit this section. He wanted to see Circle Five riders actually hazing Circle Five steers.

The fact that the bands of cattle held no cows or calves was significant in itself. Cow buyers bought only steers. Each drifting herd of Circle Five cattle that he and Tortilla Joe had seen had been composed of steers . . . and steers only.

Dawn found him hidden, watching the huge Circle Five spread below. No riders came in. Finally the cook hammered the triangle; men trooped from the bunkhouse to wash up on the long bench beside the pump before trekking into the mess shack.

Buck's glasses picked out Pincus, Jordan, Smith, Olson, and Breckinridge entering the cookshack. After breakfast, Pincus issued orders, and the riders fanned out from the ranch.

Buck quickly noticed that Jordan, Smith, Olson, and Breckinridge were not assigned jobs. The four were in the bunkhouse. Soon Rocky Pincus returned to the bunkhouse, too.

Buck realized then that the five had sneaked into

Circle Five under cover of dark, and would sleep the day away before riding out again. These men knew the northern range well. They evidently could haze steers in the intense darkness.

Buck saw Marcia Andrews ride out at noon, and again Louise Twiggs watered her roses.

The next afternoon he again met Tortilla Joe far north at their usual meeting spot.

"Sheriff Jenkins rode into Malta, like you guessed, Buckshot. He talked with the former Mrs. Matthews."

"You were in town?"

"Why not? There was no danger. Well, they talked a while. I was across the street from the woman's cafe, in a saloon, and I could see the sheriff and the woman clearly. He dug something out of his pocket and showed it to her."

"Could you see what it was?"

"They took the thing to the window. The light was better there. They looked at a gold piece."

"Money, you mean?"

"Yeah, gold money."

"How'd you know it was a gold piece? They were across the street, you say. That's quite a distance. You haven't got the eyes of an eagle."

"A man came along on their side of the street. He stopped and looked at them, then came into the saloon. He's the town drunk. He said that with that twenty-dollar gold piece he could be drunk for a month."

"What do you think about it?"

"Well, the old Mrs. Wad dug in Wad's corral, remember? And she told me she thought Wad had gold cached in the corral. I'd say she found Wad's gold."

"But where did the sheriff get that gold piece?"

"I don't know, Buck. All I can think of is that maybe the sheriff dug, too. Or found a piece of gold in the corral. And he wanted to show it to Mrs. Wad."

Buck scowled. "This has got me stumped."

"We should have dug in Wad's corral," Tortilla Joe said.

"We should have done lots of things," Buck said. "We shouldn't have ridden here, for one thing. Yeah, we'd be digging in that corral, and Sheriff Jenkins would come in behind us with his pistol out—and you'd be back in jail, waiting to get hung."

Tortilla Joe frowned. "How is a man to know where to go and where not to go, Buck?"

"You answer that," Buck said. "Where's the sheriff now?"

"About ten miles behind me, going back to Yellowstone City."

Buck studied the trail below. Sheriff Jenkins would ride along it, through trees and brush. He remembered Tortilla Joe telling how he had pulled Deputy Watson from his saddle with a rope tied between two cottonwood trees.

"Why not dump him like you did that fool deputy?" Buck asked.

Tortilla Joe's dark eyes glistened. "But what would it gain us, Buckshot?"

"I don't like him," Buck said.

"He served me bad meals when I was in jail," Tortilla Joe said. "He called me a damned Mexican. He insulted me, he did."

"He tried to keep me from seeing you," Buck McKee added. "He tried to keep you in jail forever. He tried to obstruct justice."

"We can think of lots of things that we hold against him, Buckshot, but why waste time, huh? I go string the rope?"

"Why not?"

Buck watched from the rimrock. Tortilla Joe selected a point just beyond a bend in the trail. A man could lope around the bend, ride right down on the taut rope before he saw it. . . .

Here, strong trees also bordered the trail. Buck grinned as he watched Tortilla Joe stretch his catch-rope between two box elder trees.

The rope stretched taut, and the Mexican then went down-trail, where he hid himself and his horse in the high brush. Buck looked to the northwest. Sheriff Jenkins had just come into view.

The sheriff rode at a slow trot, big hands braced on the saddle fork, his leg-tired horse covered with sweat.

Buck waved his bandana down at Tortilla Joe. The Mexican lifted his sombrero. And then Sheriff Jenkins, for some reason, swung his bronc north, riding along the rim of the coulee instead of down into it.

Hurriedly, Buck looked down the coulee. There he saw another crossing made through the brush by cattle going to water. Sheriff Jenkins had spotted that trail and would ride it; he would not ride into Tortilla Joe's trap.

Buck wondered if the sheriff could see Tortilla Joe and his horse down below in the timber along the coulee's bottom. He saw Tortilla pull back into deeper brush. That told Buck that the Mexican had seen Sheriff Jenkins skylined on the rim of the coulee.

Jenkins rode on, found the other trail, crossed the coulee, and became a dot in the distance, pushing on toward Yellowstone City. Tortilla squatted beside Buck, coiling his catch-rope.

"We haven't had a bit of luck on this range," the Mexican said mournfully.

Two nights later, Sheriff Jenkins was alone in his office, buckling on his spurs, when Buck entered, almost dragging Marcia Andrews with him.

Marcia cursed him. Her right sleeve had been pulled up, but her arm held no needle marks.

Sheriff Jenkins straightened up, pulling at his gun belt. "What're you goin' to do with her, McKee?"

"Throw her in a cell," Buck said.

Marcia screamed and tried to bite Buck's hand. No longer was she sophisticated and hard. Her red hair hung like a witch's.

Jenkins didn't seem surprised to see Buck. "On what charge?" he asked.

"Pincus and his gang are ready to move stolen cattle tonight, or I'm a Dutch uncle's monkey. And if this female saw us ride out together, she'd get a warning word to her old buddy, Rocky Pincus."

Sheriff Jenkins nodded. "I see she doesn't hit the dope. She's got no pockmarks on her arms like Old Man Twiggs and Wadsworth Matthews had. You noticed them on your friend's arm, I suppose?"

"I did." Buck studied the lawman. "You don't seem surprised to see me, Jenkins."

Jenkins tugged his heavy .45 into place. "I'm not

completely blind, McKee. You and the Mexican are experts, but a man can cut sign, you know. You came from the northeast?"

"I did. Tortilla Joe's waiting out there. Pincus and his four hands are ready to move. You rode to Fort Assiniboine, remember?"

"I did. The sheriff there will trail the sutler out when Sutton—the sutler—goes to meet Pincus and pay for the herd."

"Why do you act now? You've sat for some time doing nothing."

Sheriff Jenkins grabbed Marcia Andrews' other wrist. She kicked at him and he jumped aside.

"Louise Twiggs asked me, finally. And then I found that gold piece the ex-Mrs. Matthews had dropped when she found Wad's cache under a corral post."

Sheriff Jenkins unlocked a cell. He put the protesting Marcia Andrews in it, and the heavy lock clicked shut. "She can holler and yelp and nobody'll hear her. I don't see your point in this, McKee. They don't steal your cattle."

"Tortilla Joe's got a murder charge over him. Him and me figure one of these five killed Whitey Jordan. We might make one of them talk."

Sheriff Jenkins rubbed his hands together. "We can turn the cattle back when they enter Wishbone Canyon, just inside the reservation. They drive them that far and we got the goods on them."

"They rode out and began to drive. I rode into town for you because Tortilla Joe and I need help, and you should be there—you're the law, you know."

"You and the Mexican been pals a long time, huh?"

Buck nodded.

"I kinda suspected that. No lawyer would side a client when said client had no money. You might be making a mistake, McKee."

"What d' you mean, Sheriff?"

"Wad Matthews swore to me he didn't kill Whitey Jordan. He said the Mexican hadn't killed Whitey, either. But I had to file that warrant for Circle Five. My sworn duty, McKee."

"What're you driving at?"

"This, McKee. If we don't find out who killed Whitey, I'll have to take your partner into arrest again."

"That would mean guns, Sheriff."

"Maybe so, McKee, but I'm a sworn law officer, friend. And I got to do as my oath requires."

Buck McKee saw this squat lawman in a new light. He said, "That's between you and Tortilla Joe."

"We collect Deputy Watson and we ride," the sheriff said.

Chapter Nineteen

WHEN Buck McKee had left Tortilla Joe on the northern rimrock, there had been heat lightning playing wickedly in the south, and the storm threat-

ened to move northeast toward the bunched Circle
Five cattle being stolen.

Rocky Pincus smashed into steers, his bronc lathered, his bullwhip popping. He had one eye on the
storm to the southwest as he measured the possibil-
ities of the downpour moving into this area.

He felt a rush of cold wind, then a hot wind. That
meant the storm was moving in his direction. He
glanced at the ragged lightning, and a sudden anger
hit him. Lightning was rough on cattle—it would
make a stampede dangerous.

But if the storm came, it would hit the Circle Five
steers on the rump, driving them faster into narrow
Wishbone Canyon, the gorge that ran through the
Landry Hills onto the northwest corner of the Fort
Assiniboine Reservation.

Through the heavy blackness he saw the dark rump
of a big four-year-old steer, lumbering and slobber-
ing. Rocky Pincus's bullwhip smashed down savagely.

The animal leaped, bawling in pain, and the Circle
Five ramrod ran his black bronc in hard, the horse's
shoulder smashing against the steer's flank. Again
the steer leaped; again he bawled, and disappeared
into the darkness.

Rocky Pincus found himself on top of a long mesa
that ran east and west. He heard cattle moving
below, and mingled with bawls and the sounds of
hoofs, he heard the riflelike reports of bullwhips,
handled expertly by his four fellow cow thieves.

Rocky Pincus smiled.

He had hit upon this rustling plan immediately
after becoming Circle Five's range boss. First, though,

Old Man Twiggs had to be out of the way, but Marcia Andrews had come up with the plan—and now the owner of Circle Five lay in a comatose state, drugged until he was almost close to death.

Upon first being promoted to range boss, he had tried to play up to lovely Louise Twiggs, for many a range boss does marry the female owner of his ranch—especially if the woman is a widow. And according to Rocky Pincus's guessing, Louise Twiggs would soon be widowed.

But Old Man Twiggs apparently was made of stern stuff, because the doses of dope that would kill an ordinary man had failed to kill him. Also, Rocky's attentions had received only rebuffs from Louise Twiggs, so accordingly he had dropped his pursuit of the shapely blonde.

He raided his boss's cattle at least every three months. He had foolishly taken Wadsworth Matthews into the deal, thinking that a farmer like Wad had a lot of free time to ride range and scout for the location of the next herd.

But Wad had become a dope hound, and he talked too much, according to Marcia Andrews, under the influence of drugs. Rocky Pincus knew this was true because he had heard Wad talk in the local saloons, and the farmer had almost spilled the beans a couple of times.

Marcia had said then that Wad would have to be eliminated, or the whole thing might blow up. Rocky had agreed. Thus he and Circle Five had hit the Matthews farm but failed to kill Wad, much to Rocky Pincus's disgust.

Suddenly Rocky Pincus pulled in his bronc, a cold feeling gripping his flat belly. He dismounted and laid his ear to the ground, but he heard no strange hoofs, only the hoofbeats of the cattle and his riders off in the northern distance.

He got to his feet slowly, brushing dirt from his hands. This tall Texan—this Oliver McKee—yes, and that squat, hard-looking Mexican, Tortilla Joe . . .

The memory of the two kept haunting him, and he didn't know why, for he was sure they had left the Circle Five range by this time. Anyway, nobody had seen either of them since McKee had said he was leaving Yellowstone City.

He swung into his saddle, thinking of Sheriff Jenkins. He knew Jenkins. Jenkins appeared to be rather stupid—if you didn't know him.

He went over some points. Each fall after beef roundup, he handed in a tally sheet. That tally sheet never told the truth, but he was the only one who knew that. It always registered more Circle Five cattle than really existed.

But who could prove it false? Louise Twiggs had never questioned it. He was lucky he had a female for a boss. Women knew nothing about cattle, he felt sure.

The sore spot was still Wadsworth Matthews. Somebody had dug up Matthews's corral, even to pulling up the posts. Rocky Pincus realized somebody had been hunting for Wad Matthews's gold—gold he had received for rustling Circle Five steers.

Had the gold been found?

A raindrop hit his cheek, taking his mind from his savage musings. True to his fears, the storm was heading northeast. Another drop fell, big and hot and wet, and then another.

Chain lightning mementarily flashed, laying a coat of weird whiteness across the Montana wilderness. For one blinding second, everything stood out in a flaming tableau: the buttes crowned with black igneous rock, the jagged-cut coulees and brush, the cattle running to the northeast, and a rider to his left moving in on him.

Then the lightning died, and thunder rolled in the far distance. Rocky Pincus realized that his hand had instinctively gone to his holstered gun when he had glimpsed the rider, although he had immediately recognized the horseman as Blacky Jordan.

Blacky roweled close, his horse rearing. "They're moving good, boss," he said. "Headin' the right direction and headin' out fast. Looks like there might be a bit of rain, huh?"

"Anything suspicious?"

"Not that I've seen. Why? Should there be?"

"A man never knows, fellow. Get back to your poundin' the drags, and ride pronto."

"You need a vacation," Blacky Jordan said sourly. "Get to Butte or someplace, get drunk and spend some of your money. You've got plenty of it. Get rid of your nerves, man."

"When I need your advice, I'll ask for it," Rocky Pincus snapped. "Feed your bronc the spurs!"

Blacky Jordan turned his horse on its hind legs, his hollow laugh echoing back—and then he and horse were a dark blur moving rapidly to the north, to become lost in darkness.

Rocky Pincus swore under his breath at the hot-tempered Blacky, remembering again that he had seen Blacky shoot his brother through the heart during that stupid fight at Wad Matthews's farm.

Rocky Pincus let his thoughts dwell momentarily on Blacky Jordan. Jordan was a rat; inside, he was yellow. He put on a tough front—swaggering, gun tied low, bragging, drinking. But underneath, Blacky Jordan was a rat, and nothing more.

Pincus had met Jordan's kind before. When Jordan's kind got in a tight spot, they squealed, hollering for their lives. Pincus realized he had been wrong in taking Blacky Jordan into this gang. But a man couldn't haze hundreds of head of cattle alone. He needed riders.

He thought of Whitey Jordan. Whitey had been a tough, slow-speaking rider, fast of gun and strong of heart. Whitey had been the opposite of his brother Blacky. Maybe that was why Blacky had shot his brother through the heart?

Once again, Rocky Pincus told himself he would keep an eye on Blacky Jordan. A man never knew what he would run into, on a cow raid or off. He wondered what had become of Whitey Jordan's gold, the money paid for stolen cattle.

Blacky had probably known the location of his brother's gold cache. Blacky, in fact, might have killed Whitey just for Whitey's share of these raids. And that share, while not big for some men, was big enough for a poor cowpoke like Whitey Jordan.

Pincus would ride ahead of the herd just before it entered Wishbone Canyon, for Ike Sutton would be waiting with a man or two where the canyon spilled out onto the reservation. There he and the crooked army cow buyer would run tally on the stolen steers as they lumbered by.

By that time, the moon should be up, throwing golden light over these tumbling, endless ranges of northern Montana, and cattle could be picked out individually as they hurried by toward the butcher knives awaiting them at Fort Assiniboine's slaughter-house.

Rocky Pincus rocked his bronc in, bullwhip slashing an errant, big, white-faced, four-year-old steer across the flanks. The steer bawled and ran into the herd. Pincus coiled his whip and grinned, thinking of the Gila River spread, the one he would buy in a few years, after he had made his last raid on Circle Five.

He had scouted that area of New Mexico, there at the foot of the mountains, where the Gila, foam-tossed and clear, broke out of a canyon to move down onto the plain, pushing southwest to join the mighty Colorado at Fort Yuma.

That had been six years ago. He had pulled in his horse and studied the terrain below, eyes growing narrowed and scheming, seeing not desert and brush below but fields of alfalfa and native grass, stocked by fat white-faced cattle.

For at this bottleneck a check dam could be easily built across the Gila, diverting water into a main irrigation ditch that would run laterally along the far foothills, with side ditches spilling down to take water onto fields, the waste water then draining back into the Gila. Nature had built this spread just for him.

He had put his few cents down on the place, and then had ridden north to find cattle to steal. A waddy could never make it at thirty a month and found. He would be a poor cowboy all his life.

He wondered, idly, if he could get Marcia Andrews to go with him when the time came. There was no love between Marcia and himself, but there was a solid respect—the respect that one good accomplished thief and liar has for the other.

He stirred from his thoughts. The wind's velocity had increased; rain blew in harder. He thought of untying his black oilskin from behind his saddle, but the rain hit him so fast he was soaked immediately.

Lightning smashed across the black sky, throwing the terrain into vivid relief. Despite the cold rain, there was in Rocky Pincus a feeling of great peace.

This herd was a big one. He judged it to hold around eight hundred head, at least. Sutton paid him twenty dollars a head. That made a total of sixteen thousand for this one raid.

He kept one half of this, or eight thousand. The other eight would be divided between his four riders, giving each two thousand dollars.

They seemed content at this cut. None to date had asked for more money—except Wadsworth Matthews.

Matthews had demanded more money. He needed it to pay Marcia Andrews for his dope, he had told Rocky Pincus. Pincus had told Matthews to shake the habit, and Matthews had laughed bitterly, saying that it was impossible.

Pincus had difficulty in understanding why a man was so weak he just couldn't quit anything—women, booze, dope, cigarettes, or what have you. He had smoked since about age eleven. He had quit three years ago—just like that—and had never smoked again, nor had he had any desire again for tobacco.

He had told Wadsworth Matthews about this. Matthews had said that Rocky Pincus talked loco, and the rift between them began to widen. The break had reached its final stage when Circle Five had raided the Matthews farm with lead and fire.

Again the sourness hit Rocky Pincus's belly. He hated even to think of that raid; it had accomplished nothing; it just made things worse.

For one thing, Wadsworth Matthews hadn't been killed, there and then, as Rocky Pincus had planned. He had lived to go to the hotel, and maybe he had told Sheriff Jenkins a lot, or maybe he had kept his mouth shut.

That was the hell of it. A man' didn't know. . . .

And Rocky Pincus hadn't known that the Mexican had been visiting Wadsworth Matthews, either. If the Mexican had not been there, Circle Five could have shot down and killed Matthews in cold blood.

But one couldn't commit murder in front of a spectator like the Mexican unless one also murdered the Mexican. . . . And Rocky Pincus had been afraid to murder Tortilla Joe. Circle Five was powerful, but not that powerful.

Rocky Pincus lashed a steer across the back, heading him toward Wishbone Canyon, which was about eight miles ahead in the lightning-streaked, rain-filled night.

Gigantic chain lightning tore the clouds, followed by crashing thunder. Rocky Pincus lifted his hand and looked at it. The next lightning flash came. He had seen the life line of his hand, the lightning had been that strong.

For some reason, he thought of that tall, hard-hitting lawyer. He grinned slowly.

He had been glad when Oliver McKee had ridden on. He had been slightly afraid that McKee, if he stuck around, might have become county attorney. And McKee had been a go-getter—not dead in all directions like the present county attorney.

McKee knew how to use his fists. Rocky Pincus felt at the bump on his head, his hand sneaking under his Stetson.

McKee's gun barrel had left that bump. . . .

Chapter Twenty

THEY were in the darkness of Wishbone Canyon, the storm clouds gathering overhead, and Deputy Sheriff Isaac Watson whined: "I don't like it, Sheriff. Not one bit."

"What d' you mean?" Sheriff Jenkins demanded.

Buck McKee and Tortilla Joe were sitting on hard-breathing broncs, Buck leaning on his fork, the Mexican solid and heavy between fork and cantle.

"I'm no powder monkey, Sheriff," the deputy said.

Sheriff Jenkins lost his temper. He cursed his deputy with fervor. "You don't need to be no powder monkey, you idiot! All you have to do is light a match and put it to the fuse when I fire a shot in the night. Then you run down the canyon, understand?"

"What if the dynamite don't explode?" Watson asked.

"That's my worry, not yours."

"How come you got him for a deputy, Sheriff?" Buck said. "He's afraid of his own shadow."

"Politics," the sheriff said. "Got some pull with the county officials. But I got a hunch this is his last month as my deputy."

"You can't can me," Deputy Watson said. "The county attorney won't allow it, and my ol' uncle is a county commissioner and he might can you 'stead of me, Jenkins."

"We'll see," Jenkins said. "McKee, you ever work around black powder?"

"I haven't, but Tortilla Joe has."

"Check this deal for me, huh, Tortilla?" the sheriff asked. Sheriff Jenkins was so excited he forgot to wheeze.

Tortilla Joe dismounted. "Sonora state," he said, "when I was just a boy—about eleven. Copper mining. A *peso* a day for twelve hours' work. I bought my own grub. Of course, the *peso* was worth fifty cents *gringo* those days. Now it's next to worthless."

The Mexican lit a match, and Deputy Watson said, "My Lord, Mexican, you'll blow us all to kingdom come! Kill that match!"

"Why?" Tortilla Joe asked. "The fuse is over there. I'm over here. Yeah, this looks all right to me."

"What'll happen when the fuse is lit?" Sheriff Jenkins asked.

"There's dynamite on each side of the canyon," Tortilla Joe said. "It'll go off, of course, and throw boulders and muck down, and I'd judge this canyon would be closed almost about forty feet deep."

"Good," Sheriff Jenkins said. "You ride down the canyon when you light the fuse, Watson."

"And right into that crooked sutler's gunmen?" Watson said cynically.

"The Fort Assiniboine sheriff prob'ly has Sutton and his men under arrest by now," Sheriff Jenkins said. "Okay, McKee and Tortilla Joe. Let's ride back up the canyon."

"Going to rain soon," Buck commented.

"Let 'im come," Tortilla Joe said.

"I don't understand you," Sheriff Jenkins told Tortilla Joe. "Sometimes you speak good English. Next time you talk, you're so broken a man can hardly understand you."

"Eet ees deeficult," the Mexican said.

The trio rode out of Wishbone Canyon, coming out on the high plain that ran west. "I'll take the center," Sheriff Jenkins said, "and you take the south flank, McKee?"

Buck shrugged. "Makes no difference to me, Sheriff. I just hope I don't stop a bullet in the right place, that's all. I'd like to shovel hay to Canuck cattle this coming winter."

"We've got that to consider," the sheriff said, "but a man can't live forever, like the sky pilots say. You take the north flank, Tortilla Joe?"

"That I does," the Mexican said, "an' I hopes, too, I can feed the cattles in Canada thees weenter. An' when I rides north—if I does—I want to be free of any murder charge, 'cause next spring I weel ride south an' visit Margareeta in Chihuahua."

"Who's Marguerita?" the sheriff asked.

"One of his women," Buck explained. "Okay, men, see you later," and the lanky Texan rode south into the night.

Tortilla Joe said, "Good hunting, Sheriff," and turned his horse north, the night swallowing him and his mount. Sheriff Jenkins was alone. He had a scary feeling. In all his years in office he had never found himself in such a dangerous situation, but the Texan and Mexican seemed to take it in stride . . . a sort of everyday event to them, seemingly.

To the sheriff, Buck McKee seemed the coldest of the two, but if he could have seen Buck at that moment, the Yellowstone City lawman would have had misgivings. Buck McKee sat on his horse in the wind-driven dark, hoping that he and Tortilla Joe would live through this oncoming ruckus.

Common sense told him that Rocky Pincus, Blacky Jordan, and the other three Circle Five rustlers would fight. They hanged cow thieves in this locality, and hanged them through due process of law. And when a man faces the hangman's noose . . .

His horse back in the boulders, Buck squatted in the windbreak of a granite over-ledge, checking his .45 and his Winchester, seeing that his Colt had six cartridges in cylinder, and his Winchester's barrel had a fresh cartridge with the magazine completely filled.

He got to his feet, walked to his bronc, and put the rifle in the saddle scabbard, then jerked it free four or five times to make sure the sights didn't hang up and slow the draw down or bind the rifle tightly in the leather saddle holster.

The rain came then. It drove across the ranges, hard drops pounding; for a long moment, Buck thought it was hail, so big were the raindrops and so hard did they hit the ground. Within a minute, the Texan was soaking wet.

He made no move toward the black oilskin slicker tied behind his saddle. Unless a man strapped his pistol outside of his slicker, his draw was slow and cumbersome.

The rain was cold. It hit a man's hide and made him shiver. Buck drew back farther under the overhang, eyes north on the slight basin ahead.

He heard the oncoming stolen cattle before he saw them, although jagged chain lightning made the land as bright as day. The storm raged now, wind whistling; then, without warning, the wind suddenly fell back and died.

Now there was only the pounding of rain and the flash of lightning, followed by the rolling crash of thunder. Buck realized that the steers, boogered and scared as they were, could be easily stampeded.

He gave the situation brief thought. When Deputy Watson's dynamite roared ahead in Wishbone Canyon, the steers would just be entering that narrow defile—or so Sheriff Jenkins had planned it.

The roaring smash of the dynamite would light up the rain-filled night. Boulders would be spewed skyward. Lead steers, suddenly terrified, would wheel, tails up, and head back west toward home range, bawling and stampeding.

Buck had no interest in Circle Five cattle. It made not a bit of difference to him if Twiggs's beef was rustled or not. He wanted to find out who killed Wadsworth Matthews. But more important than that would be to find out who had really killed Whitey Jordan, if possible.

All five men on this cow-stealing expedition had been in the Circle Five bunch that had burned down the Matthews farm, and one—or more—of this group knew for sure who had killed Whitey Jordan.

How to get the men to reveal the actual killer was another problem, but Buck McKee didn't worry about that; when the time came, there would be a way. A hot iron, applied to the soles of a rustler's boots, sometimes worked miracles—even the threat of the cherry-red branding iron might bring about the needed information.

Squatting, Buck studied the cattle below, now moving toward the canyon. Tortilla Joe was somewhere north in that maze of rocks. Sheriff Jenkins would be closer to the canyon's dark maw, gaping black and ugly in the lightning.

Buck judged the herd to run around seven or eight

hundred, maybe more. Rocky Pincus, he admitted, was making money—rustling his boss's cattle and drawing down his boss's wages at the same time. And Buck thought momentarily of lovely blonde Louise Twiggs.

Marcia Andrews's goose was cooked. Sheriff Jenkins would take care of her. Old Man Twiggs's dope supply would be suddenly stopped. Sheriff Jenkins had said he would get a Malta doctor over to examine the drugged cowman.

Cattle now moved east below him. Lightning showed broad backs pushing toward Wishbone Canyon. The lead steers were about one hundred hards from the canyon's black maw when the dynamite exploded prematurely.

First, Buck saw the high roaring flash of flame. Then the roar beat across the prairie, smashing through rain. Through the flame Buck glimpsed boulders flying sky-high. The rough sides of Wishbone Canyon began sliding closed, dust rising into the rain. Then it was pitch dark.

Timid Deputy Sheriff Isaac Watson had blown off the dynamite too soon, Buck realized, silently cursing the stupid lawman as he spurred forward into the rain, short-gun up. He rammed his bronc toward where he figured Rocky Pincus would be, for the lightning had shown the Circle Five range boss pushing the drags of the herd.

For one long moment, all below was frozen in stiff review. The cattle stopped suddenly, fear grabbing them, and the riders likewise halted suddenly, staring ahead at the flames—and then violent action broke loose.

The stolen cattle lost their momentary fright. They became an instrument of stampeding destruction, heavy and deadly with long wicked horns, for they wheeled as one, then stampeded back toward their home range to the west.

Buck new that Rocky Pincus and his Circle Five rustlers were experienced hands at hazing cattle. They had known the moment the powder had blasted that the stolen steers would wheel and stampede back west.

The cowboy riding point would be in no danger. Cattle would be running away from him. But the drag and wheel cowboys were directly in the path of the stampeding beasts.

First, the steers bawled in unison. The sound drowned out the thunder momentarily. Then the hoofs began to pound the damp earth. And the earth fairly shook.

Lightning illuminated the ghastly scene—the terrified, fleeing Circle Five drag and wheel riders, the waxen, clashing horns of the steers, the hammering jar of cloven hoofs on sloppy earth. Again and again, jagged chain lightning revealed the terrible scene.

Buck saw a rider spurring his way, and he recognized Blacky Jordan. At that moment, Jordan glimpsed him. Jordan's .45 spoke, flame lancing out of the cowboy's middle as he crouched over his saddlehorn, spurring his mount for greater speed as the cattle thundered toward him.

Buck pulled in, his horse almost going over backwards. He realized that Jordan's shot had hammered into the fork of his saddle. For one moment, the Texan thought his bronc would go down, so great was the blow.

As it was, the horse went down on his hind legs, neighing in fear and terror, and Blacky Jordan shot again, whipping down on Buck. This time, Jordan missed.

Buck whirled his horse, shooting before the bronc's front hoofs were solid on soil again. Three times he shot, flame shooting into a lightning flash, and then darkness covered the range.

Jordan didn't shoot again. Buck poised on his stirrups, listening. He prayed for another lightning bolt, but none appeared.

Cattle roared west, tails up, bawling and plunging in a stream of beef. Buck listened, hoping to hear Jordan's horse running, but the roar of the cattle's hoofs was like thunder rolling across the Montana prairie.

Then lightning flashed. Long and jagged, it roared across the black sky, showing the range clearly. And Buck saw the horse of Blacky Jordan loping madly ahead of the herd, ears back and mane and tail flowing in his speed to escape death.

The horse's saddle was empty!

Buck McKee whipped his gaze back to where he had last seen Blacky Jordan in saddle. Jordan was on foot, staggering toward Buck, who was a good fifty yards away. As Buck watched, the cowboy slipped, fell forward, and lay in a heap on his belly.

Buck's bullets had caught Jordan, and Buck spurred

forward hard and fast, knowing he rode into almost certain death to save a man who but a moment before had tried to kill him, and whom he had tried to kill.

Still, he couldn't let Jordan lie there, maybe only wounded, and be killed under the hoofs of stampeding cattle. Now Buck's sorrel, running hard ahead with ears back, skimmed across the prairie toward the Circle Five man, who lay without moving, a dark spot on the wet grass.

It was a race between life and death. One misstep of the sorrel, one slip of the bronc's shod hoofs, and the cattle would be on horse and rider. Buck knew everything depended on his mount. Bent low in the saddle, he encouraged his bronc, whispering to the horse, and then, suddenly, they had reached the recumbent Blacky Jordan.

Leaning low on his left stirrup, Buck McKee's arm went down, the bronc on a dead run, the hot breath of stampeding cattle on the horse's rump.

Buck knew he would never get a chance to repeat this performance. If his clawing fingers missed snagging Blacky Jordan's gun belt, he and his sorrel could never sweep in again in an attempt to rescue the Circle Five man.

The Circle Five steers would see to that. If Buck failed to grab Blacky Jordan's gun belt, the cloven hoofs would cut the man to gory ribbons, leaving him hammered flat and bloody in the aftermath of the stampede.

Buck was aware of shooting to the west and north, but the sounds registered dully as his horse swept down on Blacky Jordan. Buck's clawing fingers caught the man's broad gun belt, then fell loose—and for a second, Buck thought he had lost.

Then his grip tightened on the gun belt, his fingers going around it. The shock almost ripped his arm from its socket, but the inert body left the ground, and, with difficulty, Buck got Blacky lying over the front of the saddle, the tough sorrel now toting a double burden. The hammering hoofs at his flank were still ready to grind him and his two riders down.

Buck felt Blacky stir. The Circle Five man was still alive. Buck held his reins with one hand, and Blacky with the other. He felt sticky blood stain the hand holding the rustler.

He drove his sorrel straight west, hoping to outrun the cattle. The horse responded gamely, running low and hard across sagebrush, and the thunder of hoofs fell behind.

Dimly, Buck realized the gunshots had died. He saw a man lying on the ground ahead, and he recognized the tough cowboy rustler named Martin Breckinridge.

Buck's heart sank. His sorrel couldn't carry three to safety. Then jagged lightning showed that Breckinridge had been shot in the head. He had to be dead with a wound like that. Buck guessed that the rustler had shot it out with Sheriff Jenkins.

Behind him, hoofs chopped Breckinridge's limp body. Buck swung gradually to the south, and then he was safe on a small hill, the stampede pouring past him to the north.

Another lightning flash showed a horse and rider trapped in the stampede. Buck recognized Jack Olson, another Circle Five rustler. Even as Buck watched, horse and cowboy went down, disappearing into the sea of mad lumbering bovines. Buck couldn't help it: he had to shudder.

For one long moment, he sat on his bronc, waiting for the next lightning flash. When it came he saw a bulky rider across the basin leading a horse toward him, and Buck recognized his partner, Tortilla Joe. His heart lifted.

Evidently, the Mexican had shot it out with a rustler, and won, for before the lightning flare died Buck was sure he saw a man tied, face down, across the saddle on the Mexican's horse.

Then darkness came in over the range. Occasionally lightning flares flashed brightly, but the storm was abating. It was moving northeast toward Canada.

Buck got Blacky Jordan down and put the man up against a boulder, its overhang keeping the rain away.

Buck's hands encountered some dried twigs and bits of wood. For years pack rats had dragged in twigs and had built a nest back in a crevice, out of the wind and rain.

Buck pulled out this debris. He touched a match to it. It was tinder-dry and immediately broke into flames, illuminating the pain-filled face of Blacky Jordan.

"I'm going to die?" Blacky asked.

"I'm no doctor," Buck said. "You got a bad bullet hole in your chest, and one just below your neck."

"I shot at you?"

"You did. Your bullet tore my saddle fork."

Sheriff Jenkins rode in with a short, black-haired Circle Five rustler, a prisoner. Buck recognized him as Smoky Smith. "I pulled him from his horse and beat him with my gun," the sheriff said, forgetting to wheeze. "He shot at me six times and missed. This was my lucky night."

Deputy Sheriff Isaac Watson rode in, dismounted, and said, "I shot the powder off at the right time, huh?"

Sheriff Jenkins took two big strides. He faced Watson, who threw up a defensive arm—too late. The sheriff's fist collided with Watson's jaw.

Watson walked backwards, hit a rock, and sat down, his head hitting a boulder behind him. The blow knocked him out. Watson rolled on his left side and was motionless.

"Hope I didn't kill him," the sheriff said. He felt Watson's throat. "Nah, his heart's hammerin' like a new pump. He's the dumbest man I've ever seen."

"You should look twice at me," Buck said.

"Huh?" the sheriff asked, now wheezing.

Tortilla Joe rode in. He had a struggling Rocky Pincus tied to the saddle of his horse. "He isn't a very good shot," the Mexican said. "Six times he shot at me and missed me every time."

"I don't see any blood on him," Buck exclaimed.

"His gun went empty. I chased him down when he tried to load. I jumped on him and here we are."

"Seems to me your bottom lip is twice as big as normal," Buck said.

Tortilla Joe touched his swollen lip. "He hit me with a right. I can't fist-fight like I used to. I guess I grow old, huh?"

"It comes to every human," Buck said.

Two hours later, Buck and Tortilla Joe rode north, heading for Canada. Tortilla Joe was freed of the murder charge. Blacky Jordan, before he died, had admitted killing his brother. The dying gunman had also stated that Rocky Pincus had sneaked up the back stairway of the hotel to murder Matthews.

At this statement, Pincus had lost his head and tried to get at the dying man, who taunted him. Without knowing what he really said in his rage, Rocky Pincus admitted he had killed Wadsworth Matthews.

Sheriff Jenkins had witnesses other than Deputy Sheriff Watson, for the Fort Assiniboine sheriff had ridden in with sutler Ike Sutton and his riders as prisoners.

"We got off lucky, *amigo*," Tortilla Joe said. "I got no bullet holes in me. You only got the fork of your saddle ruined, and Sheriff Jenkins said the county would send you a check in Canada."

Dawn was tiptoeing over the magnificent northern range, lighting the high buttes to the east with golden glory. Bewhiskered Buck McKee rubbed his jaw. "Only one thing I don't know," he said.

"And that, partner?"

"Who slugged me outside the Antlers Cafe."

Tortilla Joe looked at his partner. "Does it make any difference now?"

"Not now," Buck said, and he laughed.